My Little Pony

Adventures in Friendship

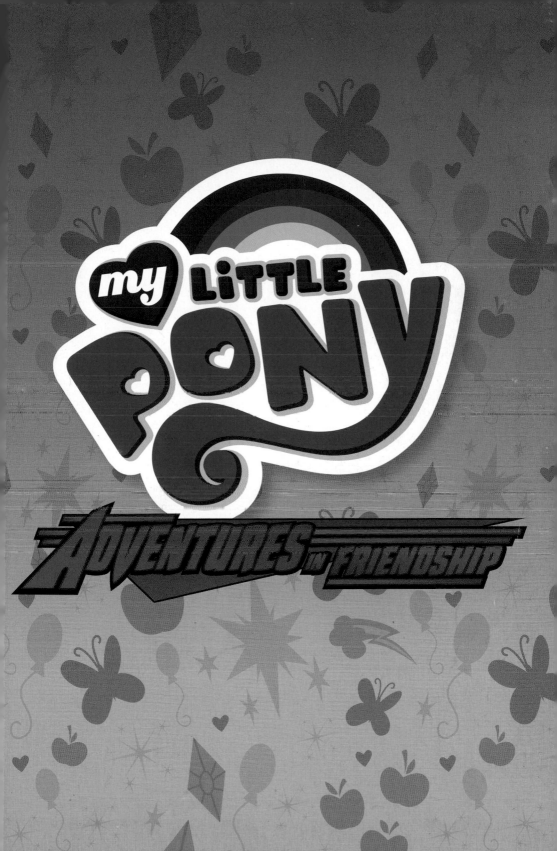

COVER BY **SARA RICHARD**

COLLECTION EDITS BY **JUSTIN EISINGER** AND **ALONZO SIMON**

COLLECTION DESIGN BY **THOM ZAHLER**

Special thanks to Erin Comella, Robert Fewkes, Joe Furfaro, Heather Hopkins, Pat Jarret, Ed Lane, Brian Lenard, Marissa Mansolillo, Donna Tobin, Michael Vogel, and Michael Kelly for their invaluable assistance.

ISBN: 978-1-63140-225-8

18 17 16 15   1 2 3 4

IDW® Licensed By: *Hasbro*

www.IDWPUBLISHING.com

IDW founded by Ted Adams, Alex Garner, Kris Oprisko, and Robbie Robbins

Ted Adams, CEO & Publisher
Greg Goldstein, President & COO
Robbie Robbins, EVP/Sr. Graphic Artist
Chris Ryall, Chief Creative Officer/Editor-in-Chief
Matthew Ruzicka, CPA, Chief Financial Officer
Alan Payne, VP of Sales
Dirk Wood, VP of Marketing
Lorelei Bunjes, VP of Digital Services
Jeff Webber, VP of Digital Publishing & Business Development

Facebook: **facebook.com/idwpublishing**
Twitter: **@idwpublishing**
YouTube: **youtube.com/idwpublishing**
Instagram: **instagram.com/idwpublishing**
deviantART: **idwpublishing.deviantart.com**
Pinterest: **pinterest.com/idwpublishing/idw-staff-faves**

Originally published as MY LITTLE PONY MICRO-SERIES #5: PINKIE PIE, MY LITTLE PONY MICRO-SERIES #6: APPLEJACK, and MY LITTLE PONY: FRIENDS FOREVER #1.

CHAPTER ONE

PINKIE PIE
WRITTEN BY **TED ANDERSON**
ART AND COLORS BY **BEN BATES**
LETTERS BY **NEIL UYETAKE**

APPLEJACK
WRITTEN BY **BOBBY CURNOW**
ART AND LYRICS BY **BRENDA HICKEY**
COLORS BY **HEATHER BRECKEL**
LETTERS BY **NEIL UYETAKE**

CHAPTER TWO

CHAPTER THREE

PINKIE PIE AND APPLEJACK
WRITTEN AND LETTERED BY **ALEX DE CAMPI**
ART BY **CARLA SPEED MCNEIL**
COLORS BY **JENN MANLEY LEE**
AND **BILL MUDRON**

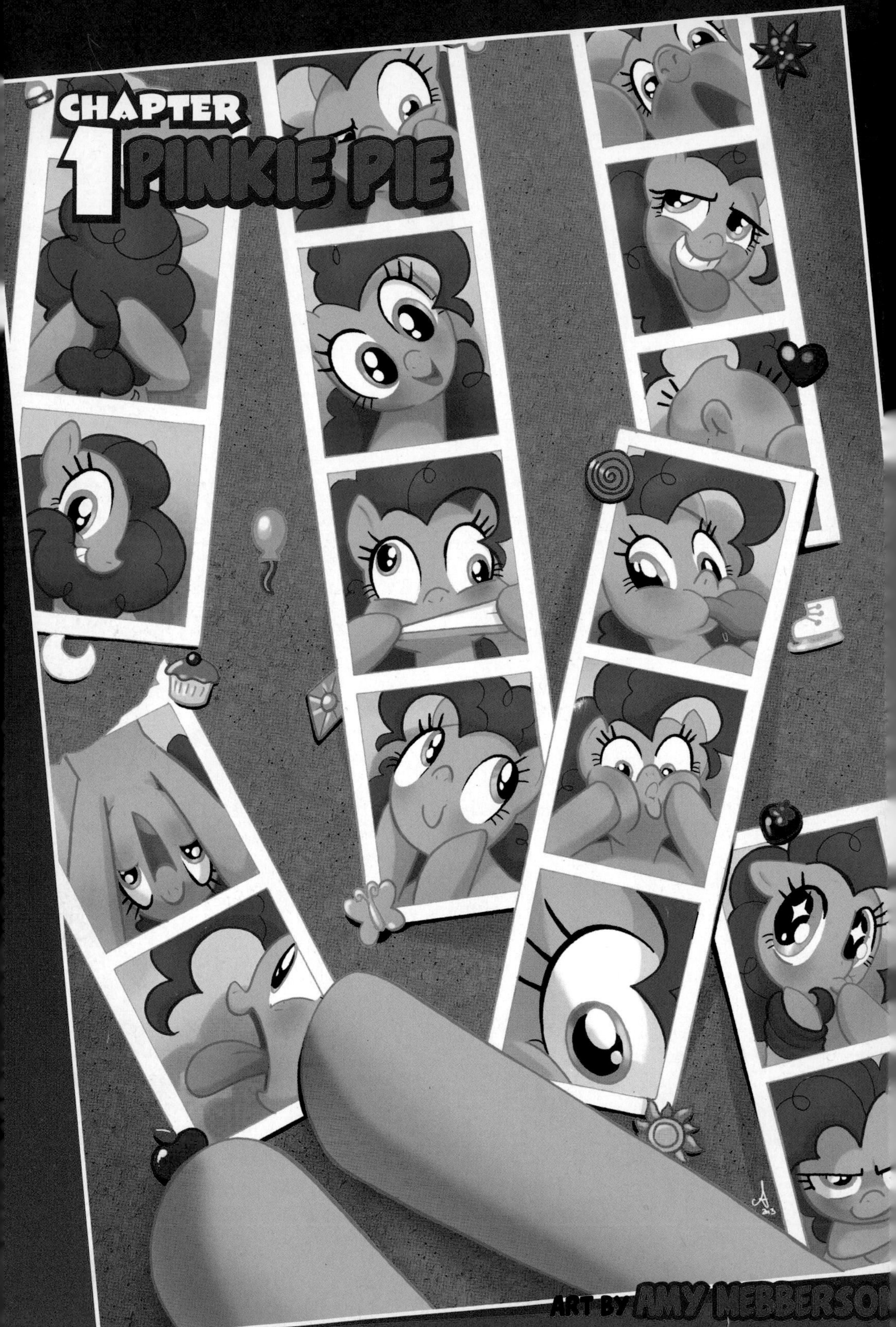

CHAPTER 1 PINKIE PIE
ART BY AMY MEBBERSON

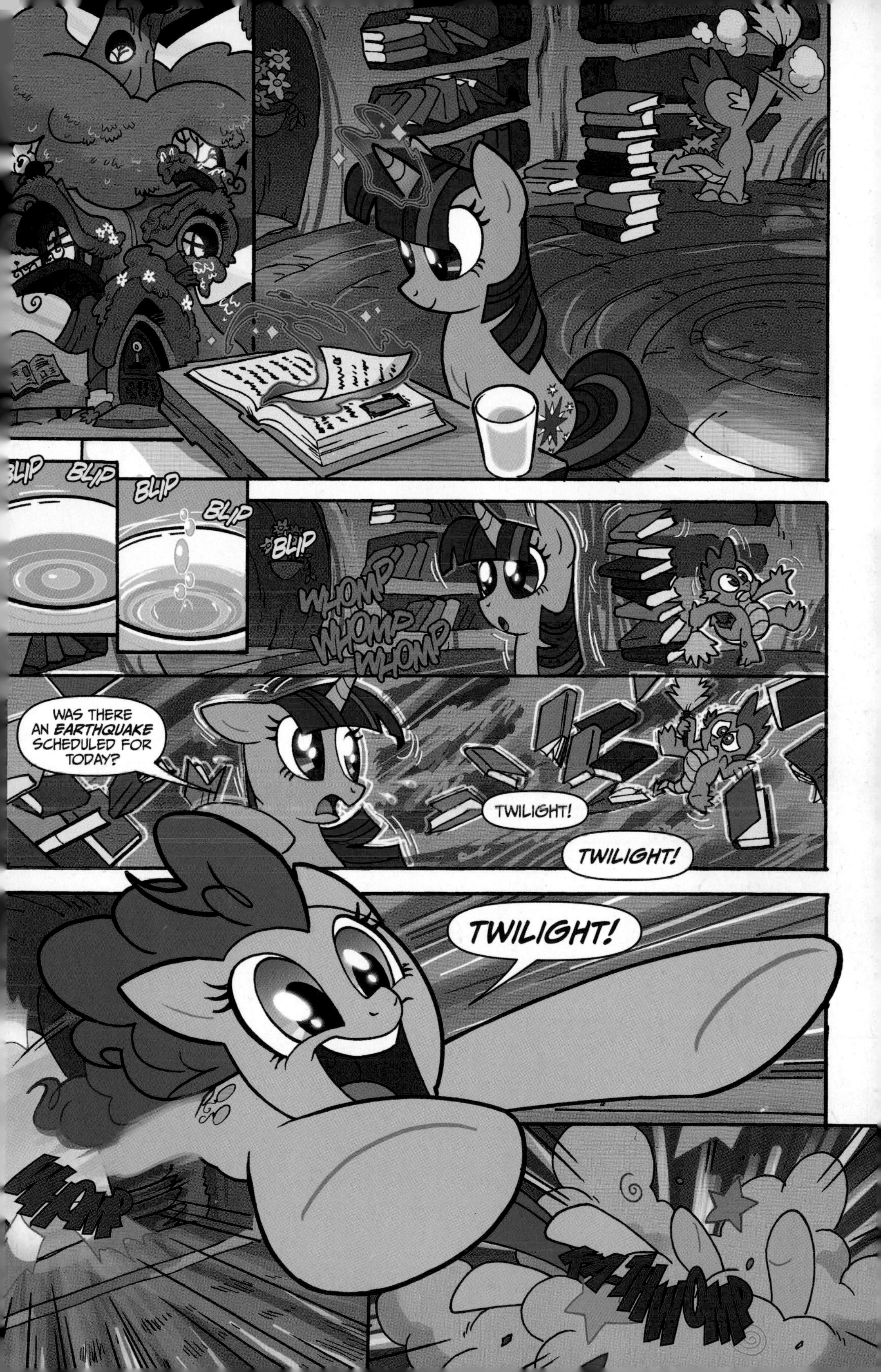
BLIP
BLIP
BLIP
BLIP
BLIP
WHOMP
WHOMP
WHOMP
WAS THERE AN EARTHQUAKE SCHEDULED FOR TODAY?
TWILIGHT!
TWILIGHT!
TWILIGHT!
WHOMP

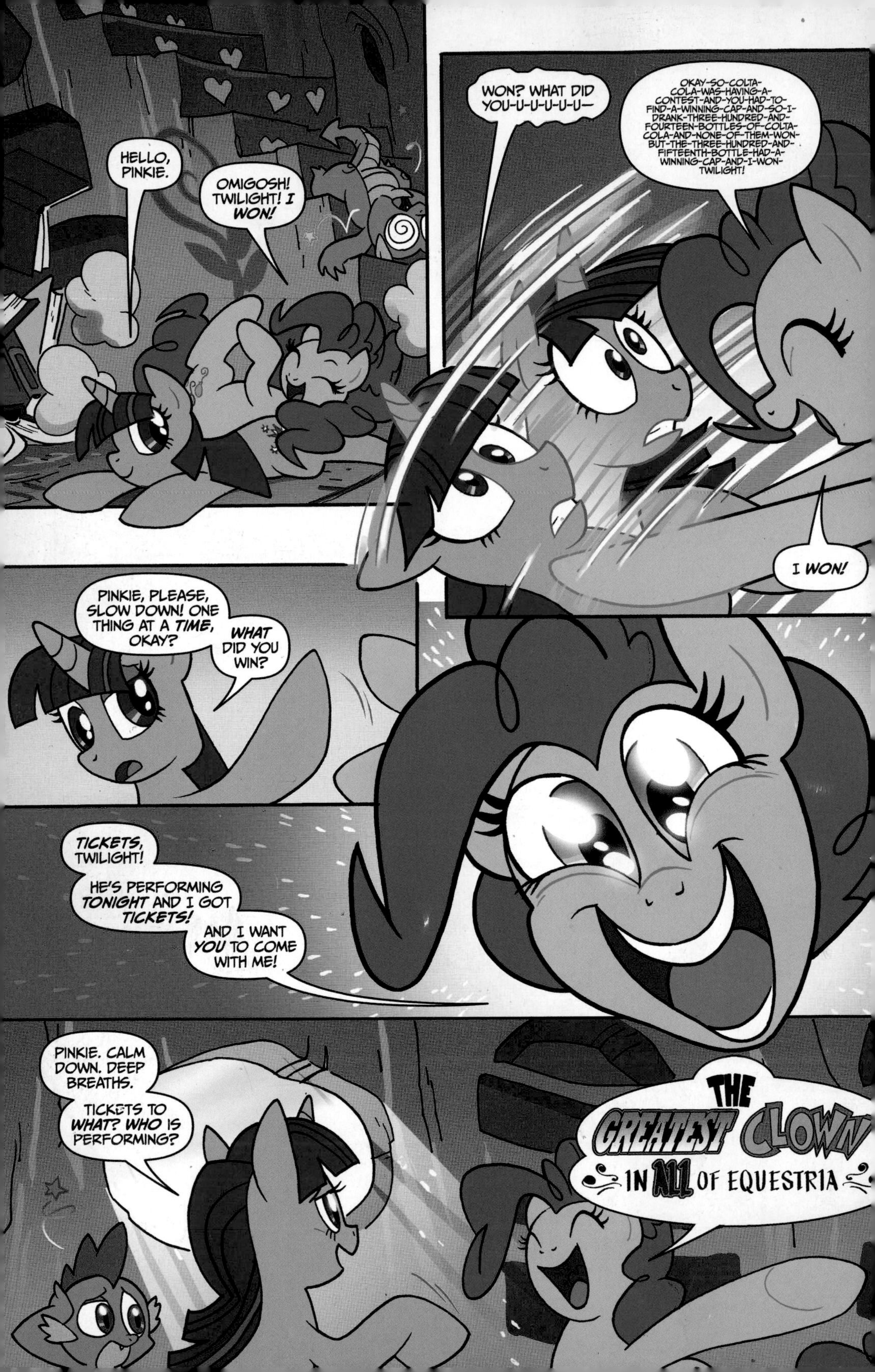
HELLO, PINKIE.
OMIGOSH! TWILIGHT! I WON!
WON? WHAT DID YOU-U-U-U-U-U—
OKAY-SO-COLTA-COLA-WAS-HAVING-A-CONTEST-AND-YOU-HAD-TO-FIND-A-WINNING-CAP-AND-SO-I-DRANK-THREE-HUNDRED-AND-FOURTEEN-BOTTLES-OF-COLTA-COLA-AND-NONE-OF-THEM-WON-BUT-THE-THREE-HUNDRED-AND-FIFTEENTH-BOTTLE-HAD-A-WINNING-CAP-AND-I-WON-TWILIGHT!
I WON!
PINKIE, PLEASE, SLOW DOWN! ONE THING AT A TIME, OKAY?
WHAT DID YOU WIN?
TICKETS, TWILIGHT!
HE'S PERFORMING TONIGHT AND I GOT TICKETS!
AND I WANT YOU TO COME WITH ME!
PINKIE. CALM DOWN. DEEP BREATHS.
TICKETS TO WHAT? WHO IS PERFORMING?
THE GREATEST CLOWN IN ALL OF EQUESTRIA

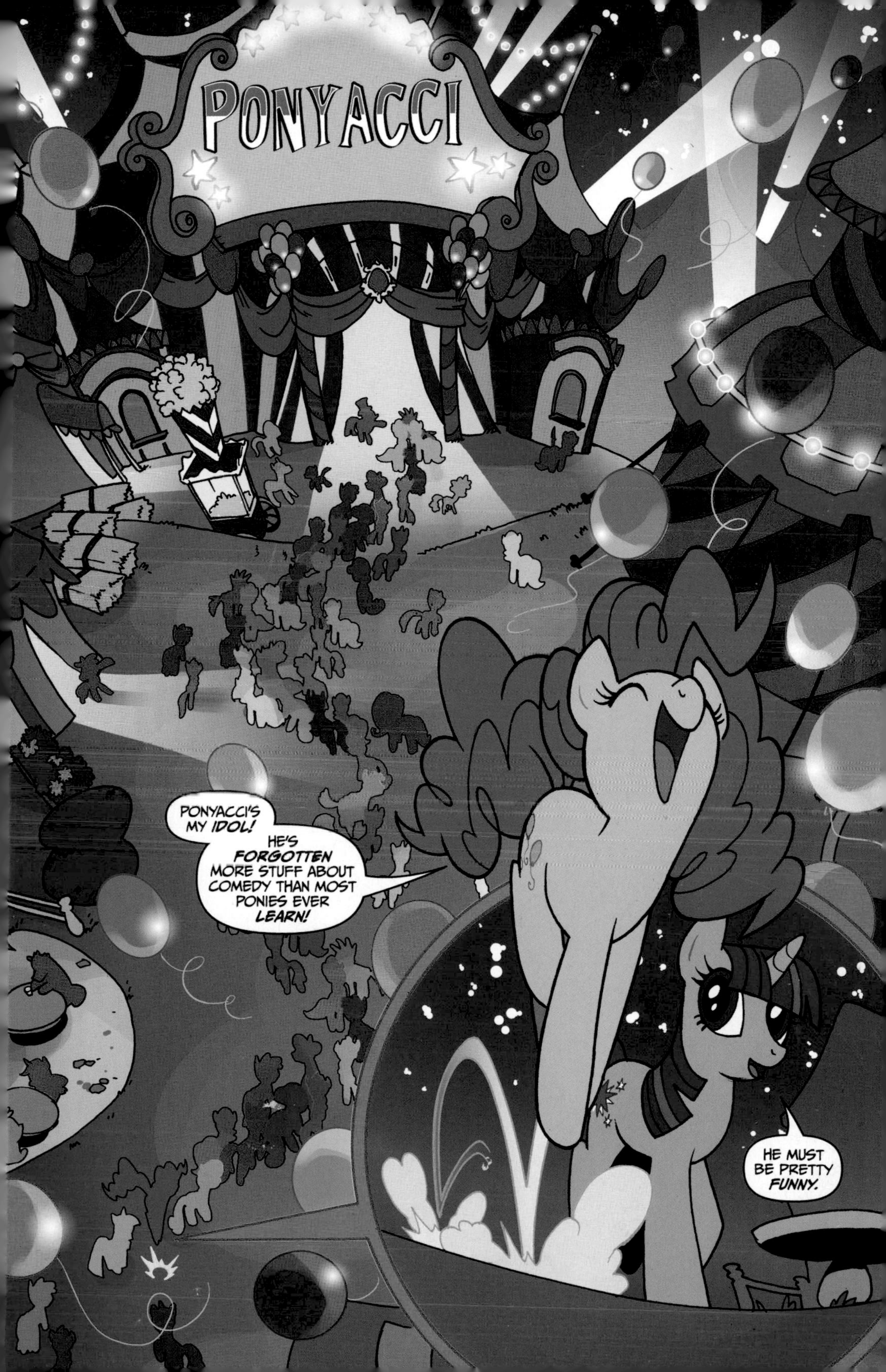
PONYACCI
PONYACCI'S MY *IDOL!*
HE'S *FORGOTTEN* MORE STUFF ABOUT COMEDY THAN MOST PONIES EVER *LEARN!*
HE MUST BE PRETTY *FUNNY.*

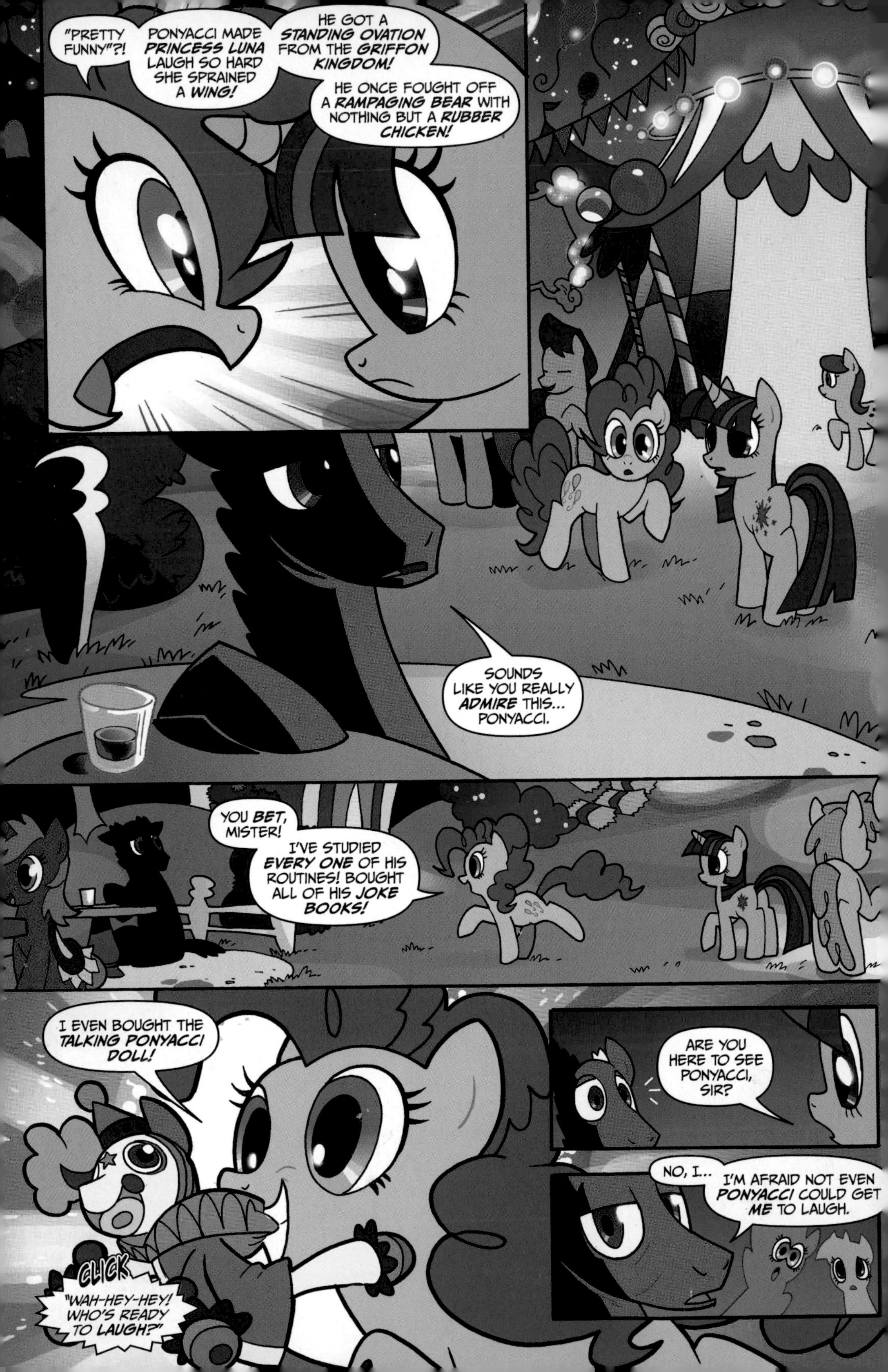
"PRETTY FUNNY"?!
PONYACCI MADE PRINCESS LUNA LAUGH SO HARD SHE SPRAINED A WING!
HE GOT A STANDING OVATION FROM THE GRIFFON KINGDOM!
HE ONCE FOUGHT OFF A RAMPAGING BEAR WITH NOTHING BUT A RUBBER CHICKEN!
SOUNDS LIKE YOU REALLY ADMIRE THIS... PONYACCI.
YOU BET, MISTER!
I'VE STUDIED EVERY ONE OF HIS ROUTINES! BOUGHT ALL OF HIS JOKE BOOKS!
I EVEN BOUGHT THE TALKING PONYACCI DOLL!
CLICK
"WAH-HEY-HEY! WHO'S READY TO LAUGH?"
ARE YOU HERE TO SEE PONYACCI, SIR?
NO, I...
I'M AFRAID NOT EVEN PONYACCI COULD GET ME TO LAUGH.

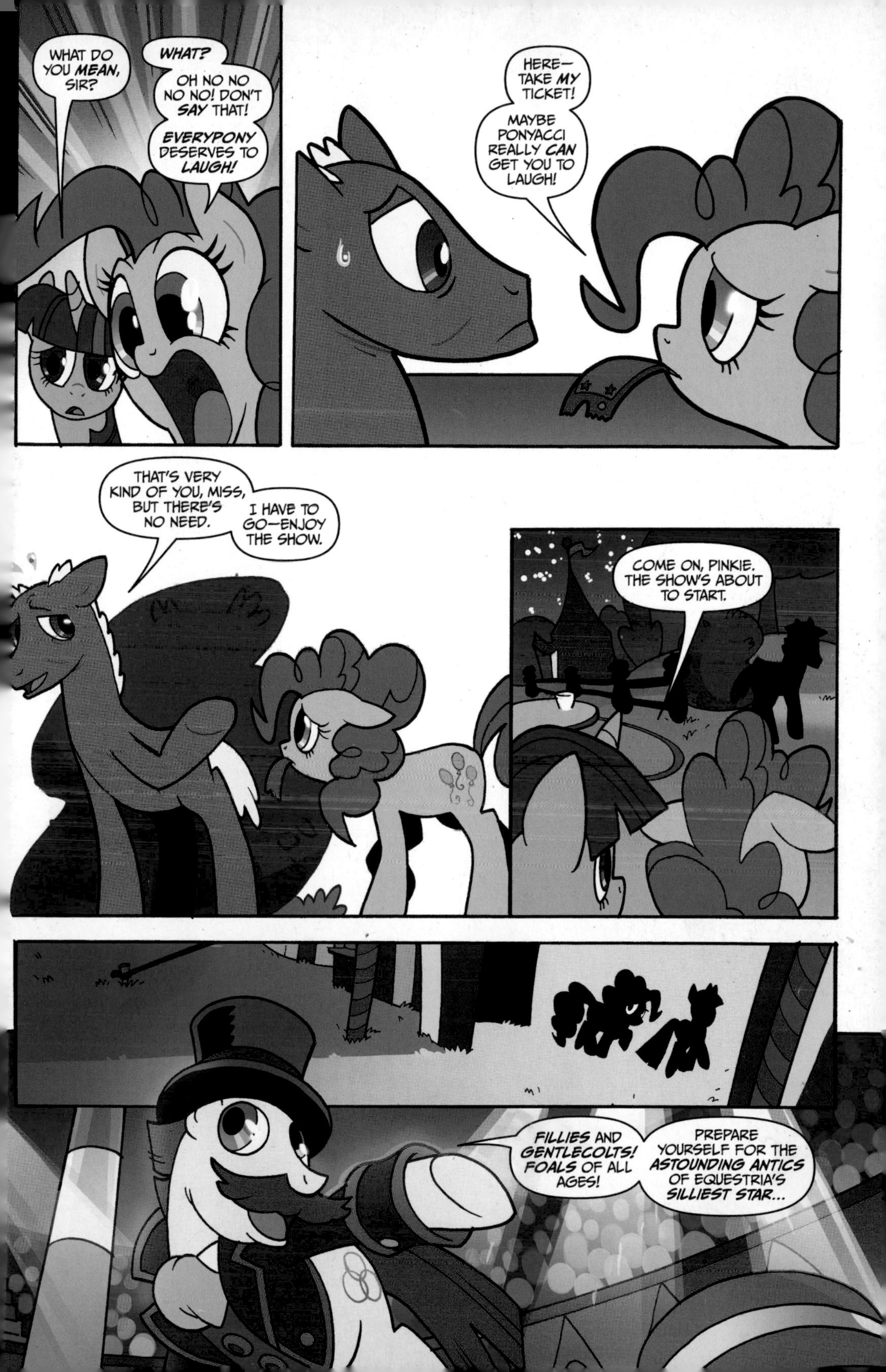
WHAT DO YOU MEAN, SIR?
WHAT?
OH NO NO NO NO! DON'T SAY THAT!
EVERYPONY DESERVES TO LAUGH!
HERE— TAKE MY TICKET!
MAYBE PONYACCI REALLY CAN GET YOU TO LAUGH!
THAT'S VERY KIND OF YOU, MISS, BUT THERE'S NO NEED.
I HAVE TO GO—ENJOY THE SHOW.
COME ON, PINKIE. THE SHOW'S ABOUT TO START.
FILLIES AND GENTLECOLTS! FOALS OF ALL AGES!
PREPARE YOURSELF FOR THE ASTOUNDING ANTICS OF EQUESTRIA'S SILLIEST STAR...

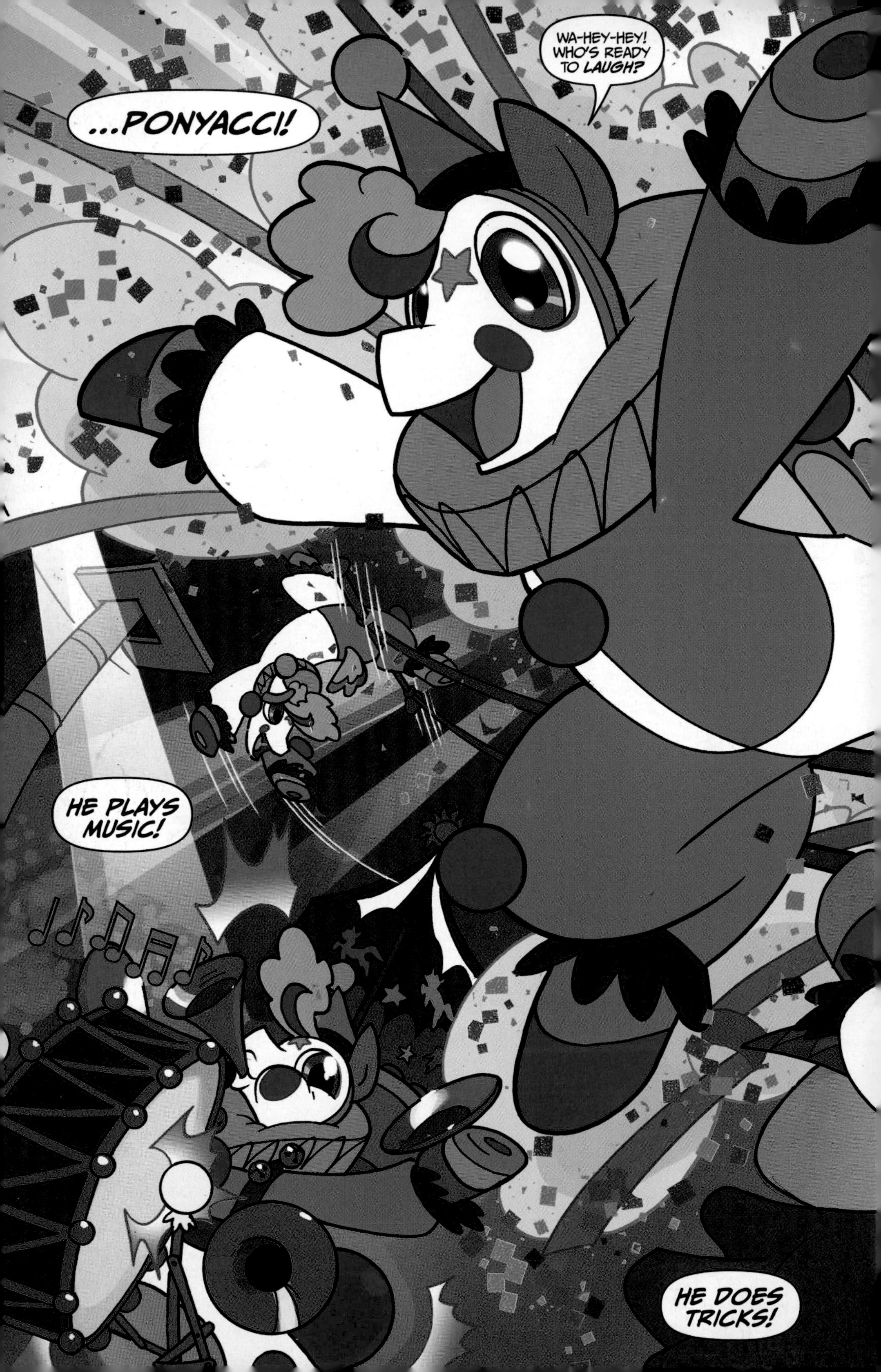
...PONYACCI!
WA-HEY-HEY! WHO'S READY TO LAUGH?
HE PLAYS MUSIC!
HE DOES TRICKS!

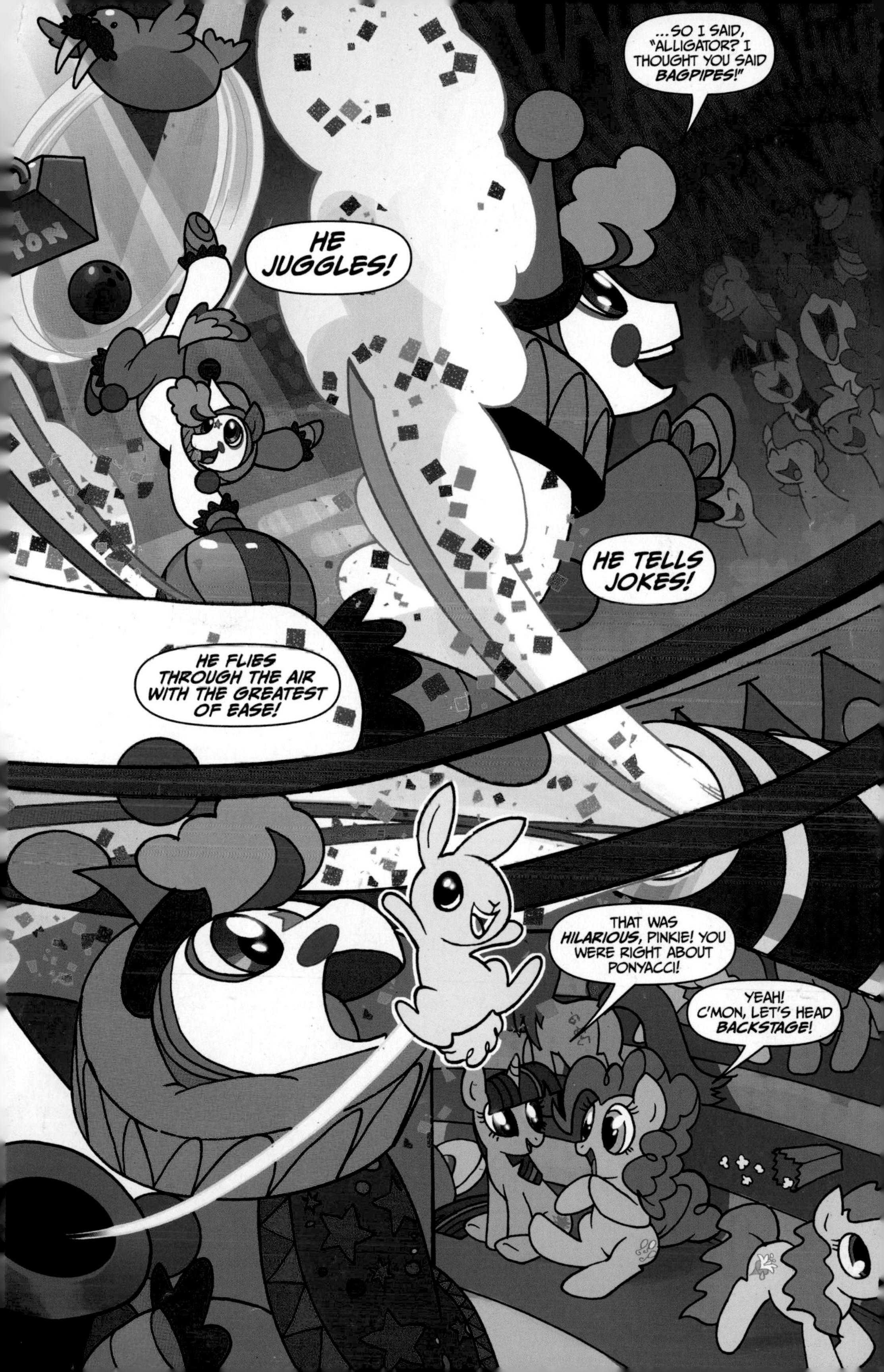
...SO I SAID, "ALLIGATOR? I THOUGHT YOU SAID BAGPIPES!"
HE JUGGLES!
HE TELLS JOKES!
HE FLIES THROUGH THE AIR WITH THE GREATEST OF EASE!
THAT WAS HILARIOUS, PINKIE! YOU WERE RIGHT ABOUT PONYACCI!
YEAH! C'MON, LET'S HEAD BACKSTAGE!

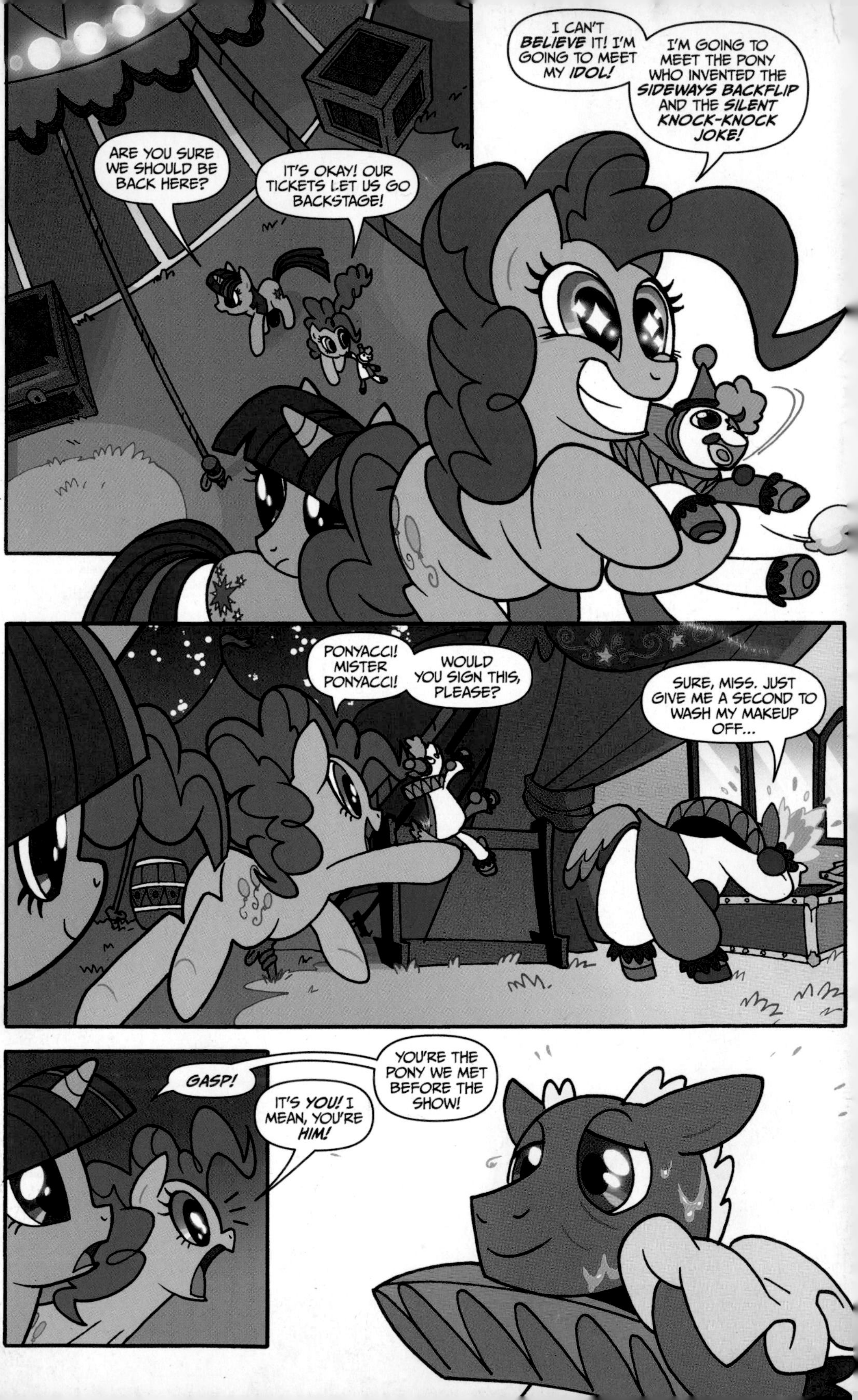
ARE YOU SURE WE SHOULD BE BACK HERE?
IT'S OKAY! OUR TICKETS LET US GO BACKSTAGE!
I CAN'T ***BELIEVE*** IT! I'M GOING TO MEET MY ***IDOL!***
I'M GOING TO MEET THE PONY WHO INVENTED THE ***SIDEWAYS BACKFLIP*** AND THE ***SILENT KNOCK-KNOCK JOKE!***
PONYACCI! MISTER PONYACCI!
WOULD YOU SIGN THIS, PLEASE?
SURE, MISS. JUST GIVE ME A SECOND TO WASH MY MAKEUP OFF...
GASP!
IT'S ***YOU!*** I MEAN, YOU'RE ***HIM!***
YOU'RE THE PONY WE MET BEFORE THE SHOW!

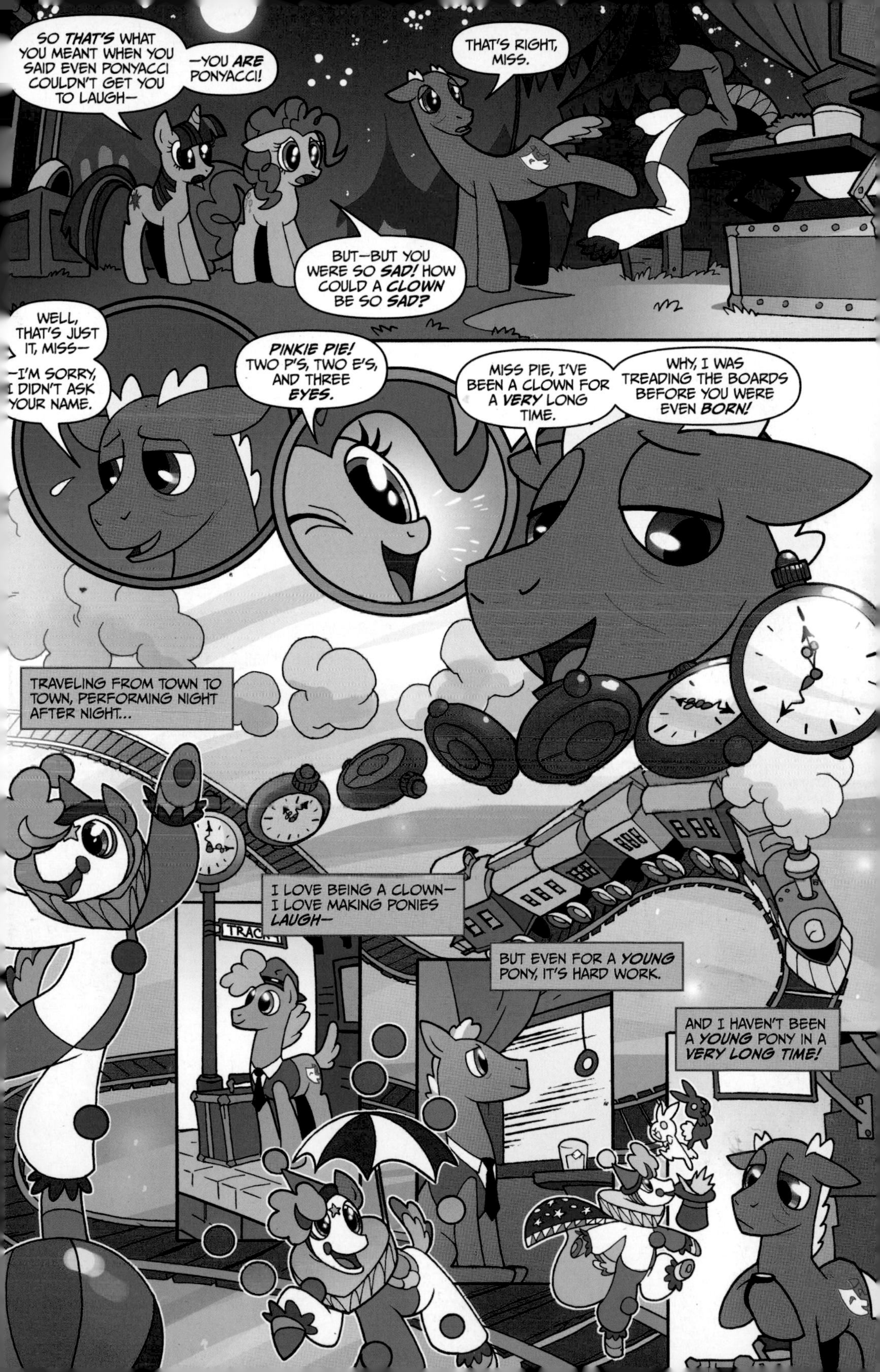
SO THAT'S WHAT YOU MEANT WHEN YOU SAID EVEN PONYACCI COULDN'T GET YOU TO LAUGH—
—YOU ARE PONYACCI!
THAT'S RIGHT, MISS.
BUT—BUT YOU WERE SO SAD! HOW COULD A CLOWN BE SO SAD?
WELL, THAT'S JUST IT, MISS—
—I'M SORRY, I DIDN'T ASK YOUR NAME.
PINKIE PIE! TWO P'S, TWO E'S, AND THREE EYES.
MISS PIE, I'VE BEEN A CLOWN FOR A VERY LONG TIME.
WHY, I WAS TREADING THE BOARDS BEFORE YOU WERE EVEN BORN!
TRAVELING FROM TOWN TO TOWN, PERFORMING NIGHT AFTER NIGHT...
I LOVE BEING A CLOWN— I LOVE MAKING PONIES LAUGH—
TRACK 1
BUT EVEN FOR A YOUNG PONY, IT'S HARD WORK.
AND I HAVEN'T BEEN A YOUNG PONY IN A VERY LONG TIME!

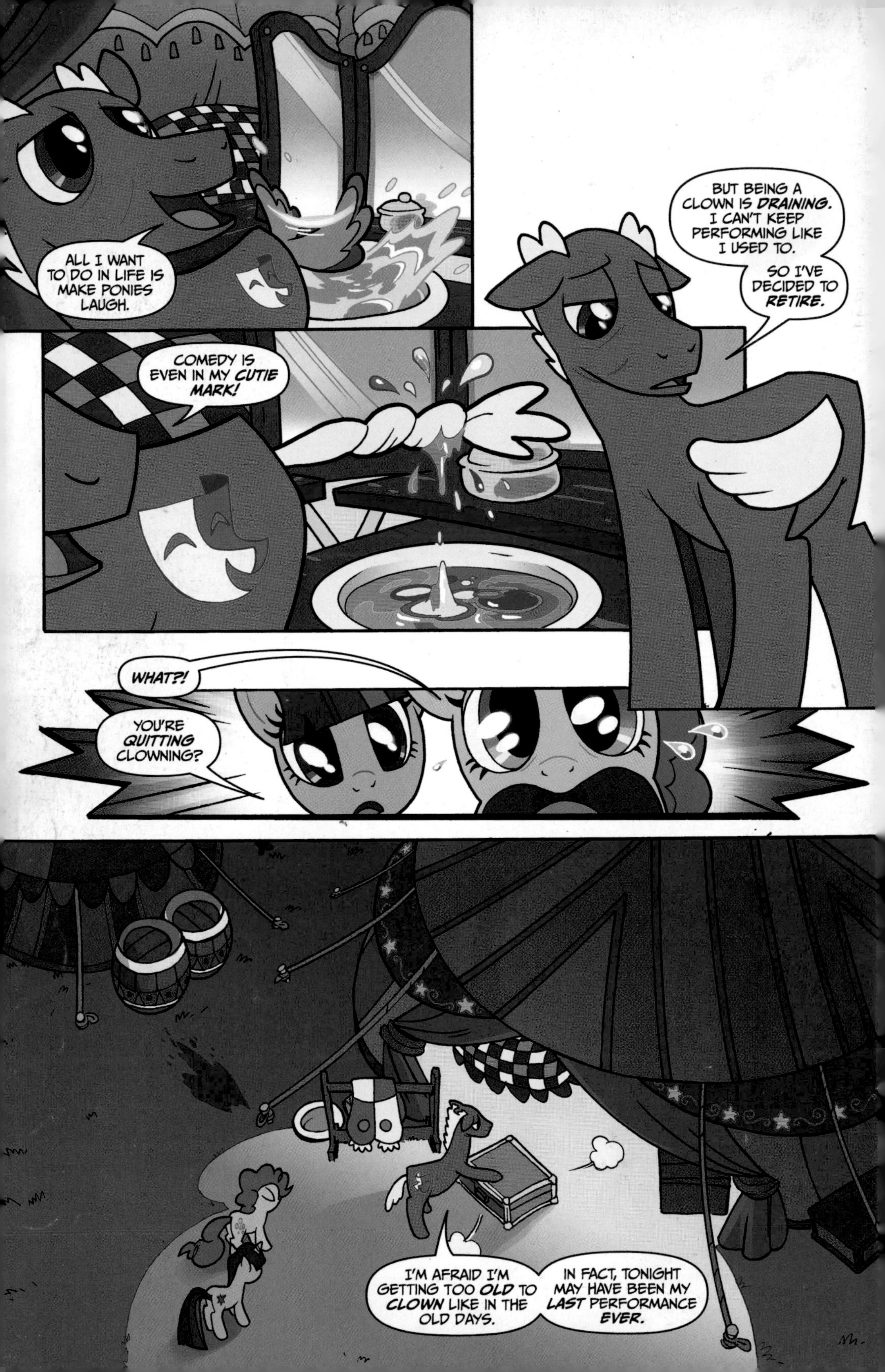
ALL I WANT TO DO IN LIFE IS MAKE PONIES LAUGH.
COMEDY IS EVEN IN MY CUTIE MARK!
BUT BEING A CLOWN IS DRAINING. I CAN'T KEEP PERFORMING LIKE I USED TO.
SO I'VE DECIDED TO RETIRE.
WHAT?!
YOU'RE QUITTING CLOWNING?
I'M AFRAID I'M GETTING TOO OLD TO CLOWN LIKE IN THE OLD DAYS.
IN FACT, TONIGHT MAY HAVE BEEN MY LAST PERFORMANCE EVER.

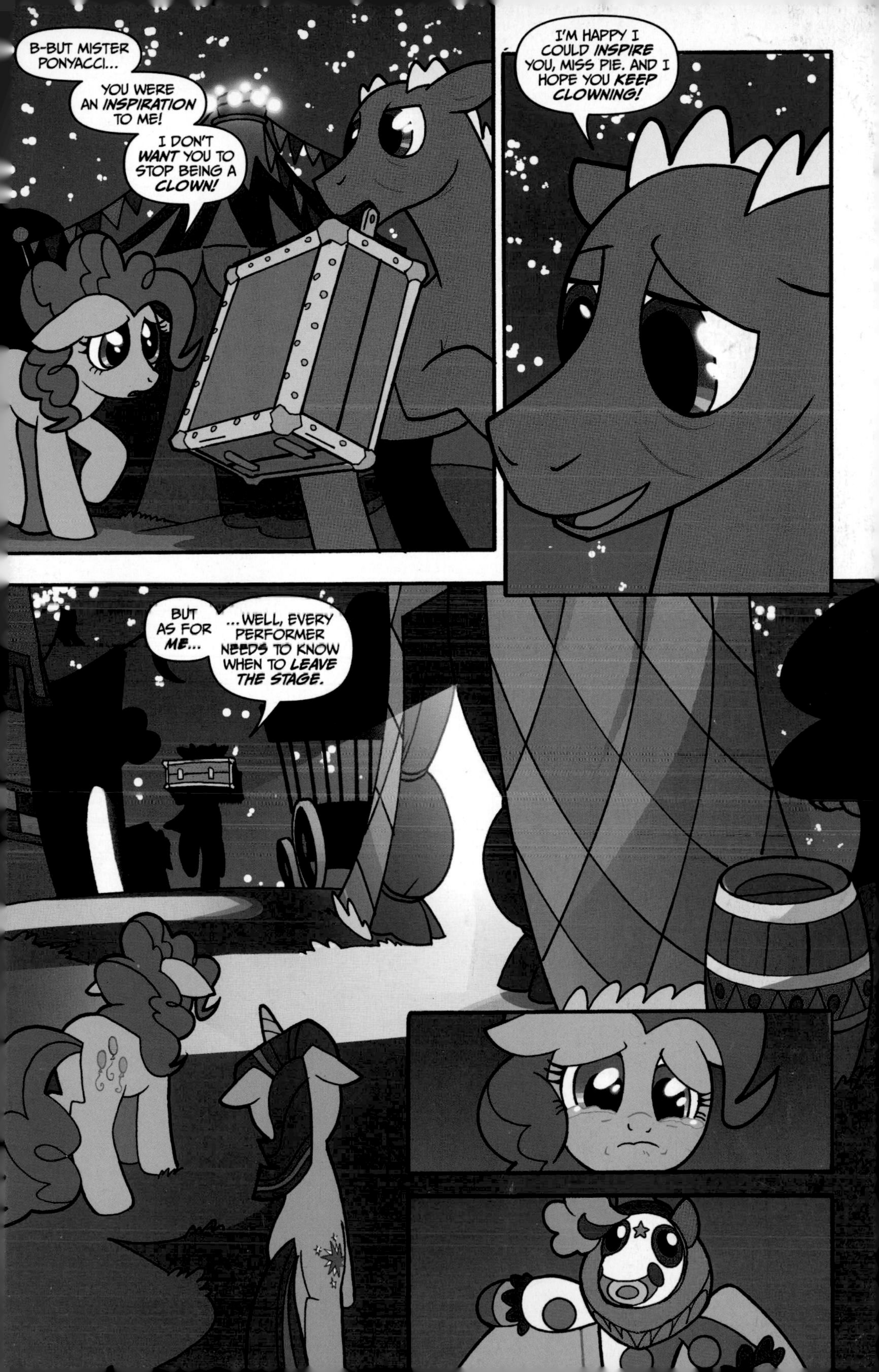
B-BUT MISTER PONYACCI...
YOU WERE AN INSPIRATION TO ME!
I DON'T WANT YOU TO STOP BEING A CLOWN!
I'M HAPPY I COULD INSPIRE YOU, MISS PIE. AND I HOPE YOU KEEP CLOWNING!
BUT AS FOR ME...
...WELL, EVERY PERFORMER NEEDS TO KNOW WHEN TO LEAVE THE STAGE.

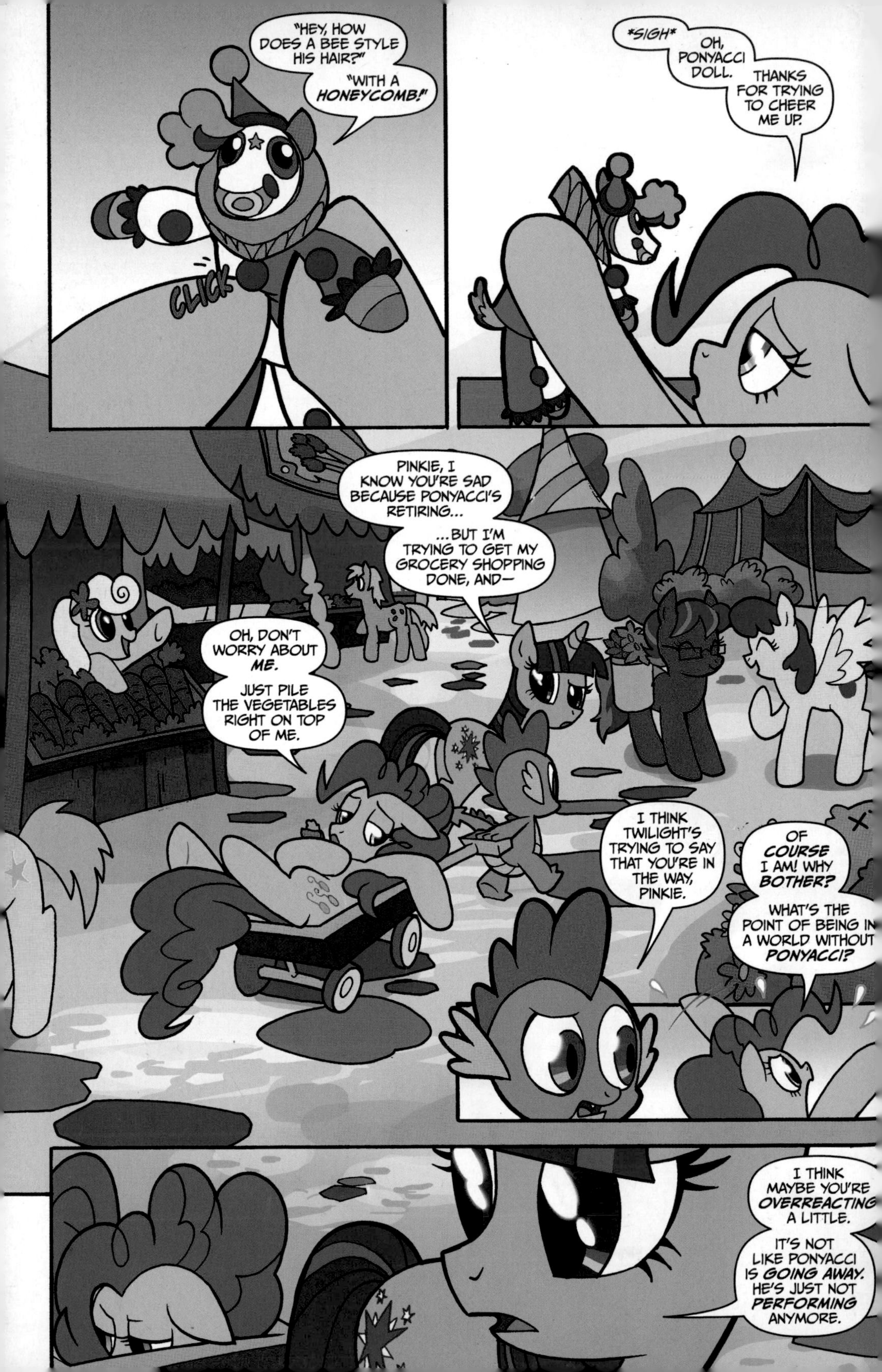
"HEY, HOW DOES A BEE STYLE HIS HAIR?"
"WITH A HONEYCOMB!"
CLICK
SIGH OH, PONYACCI DOLL.
THANKS FOR TRYING TO CHEER ME UP.
PINKIE, I KNOW YOU'RE SAD BECAUSE PONYACCI'S RETIRING...
...BUT I'M TRYING TO GET MY GROCERY SHOPPING DONE, AND—
OH, DON'T WORRY ABOUT ME.
JUST PILE THE VEGETABLES RIGHT ON TOP OF ME.
I THINK TWILIGHT'S TRYING TO SAY THAT YOU'RE IN THE WAY, PINKIE.
OF COURSE I AM! WHY BOTHER?
WHAT'S THE POINT OF BEING IN A WORLD WITHOUT PONYACCI?
I THINK MAYBE YOU'RE OVERREACTING A LITTLE.
IT'S NOT LIKE PONYACCI IS GOING AWAY. HE'S JUST NOT PERFORMING ANYMORE.

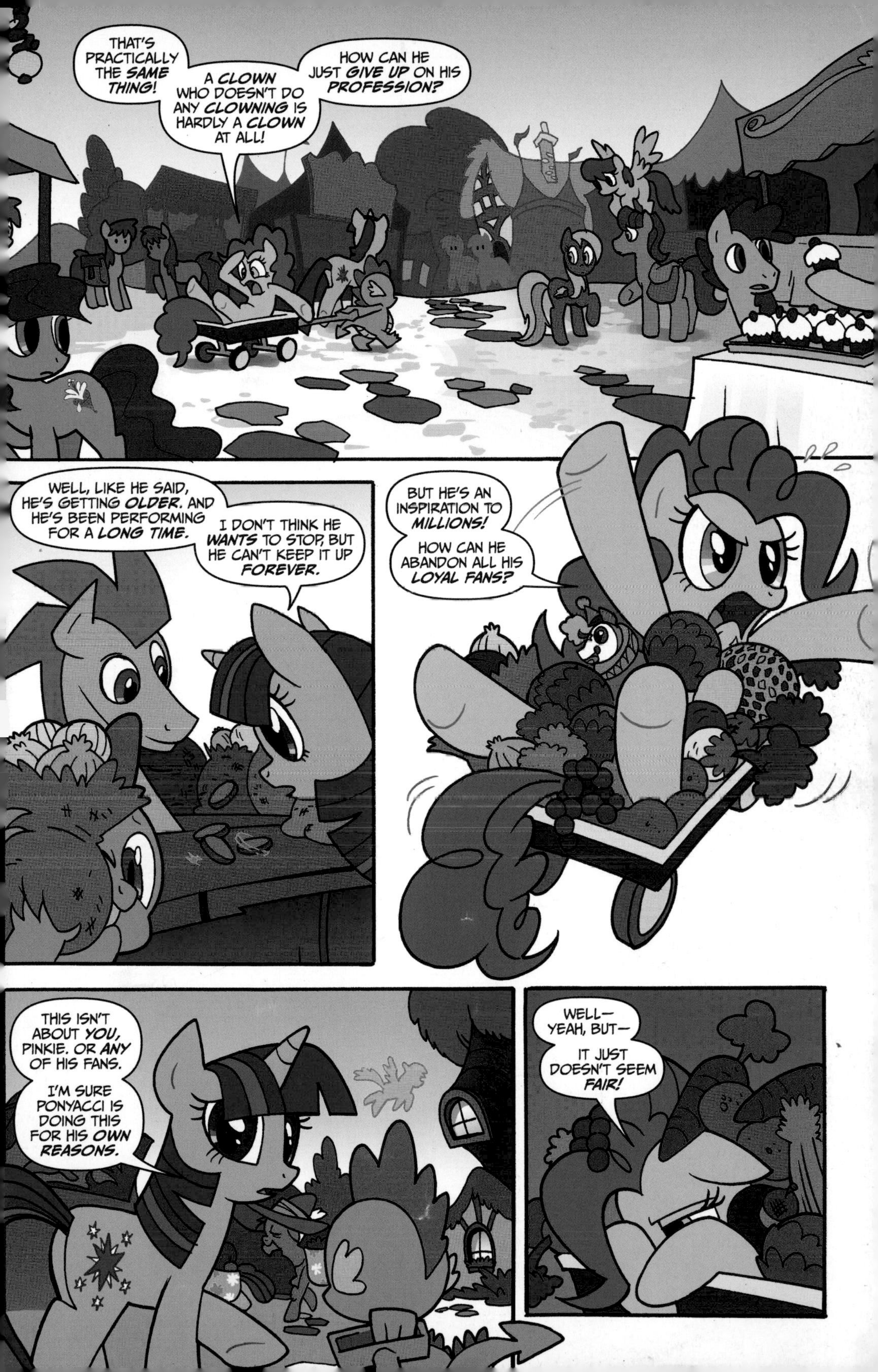

THAT'S PRACTICALLY THE SAME THING!
A CLOWN WHO DOESN'T DO ANY CLOWNING IS HARDLY A CLOWN AT ALL!
HOW CAN HE JUST GIVE UP ON HIS PROFESSION?
WELL, LIKE HE SAID, HE'S GETTING OLDER. AND HE'S BEEN PERFORMING FOR A LONG TIME.
I DON'T THINK HE WANTS TO STOP, BUT HE CAN'T KEEP IT UP FOREVER.
BUT HE'S AN INSPIRATION TO MILLIONS!
HOW CAN HE ABANDON ALL HIS LOYAL FANS?
THIS ISN'T ABOUT YOU, PINKIE. OR ANY OF HIS FANS.
I'M SURE PONYACCI IS DOING THIS FOR HIS OWN REASONS.
WELL— YEAH, BUT—
IT JUST DOESN'T SEEM FAIR!

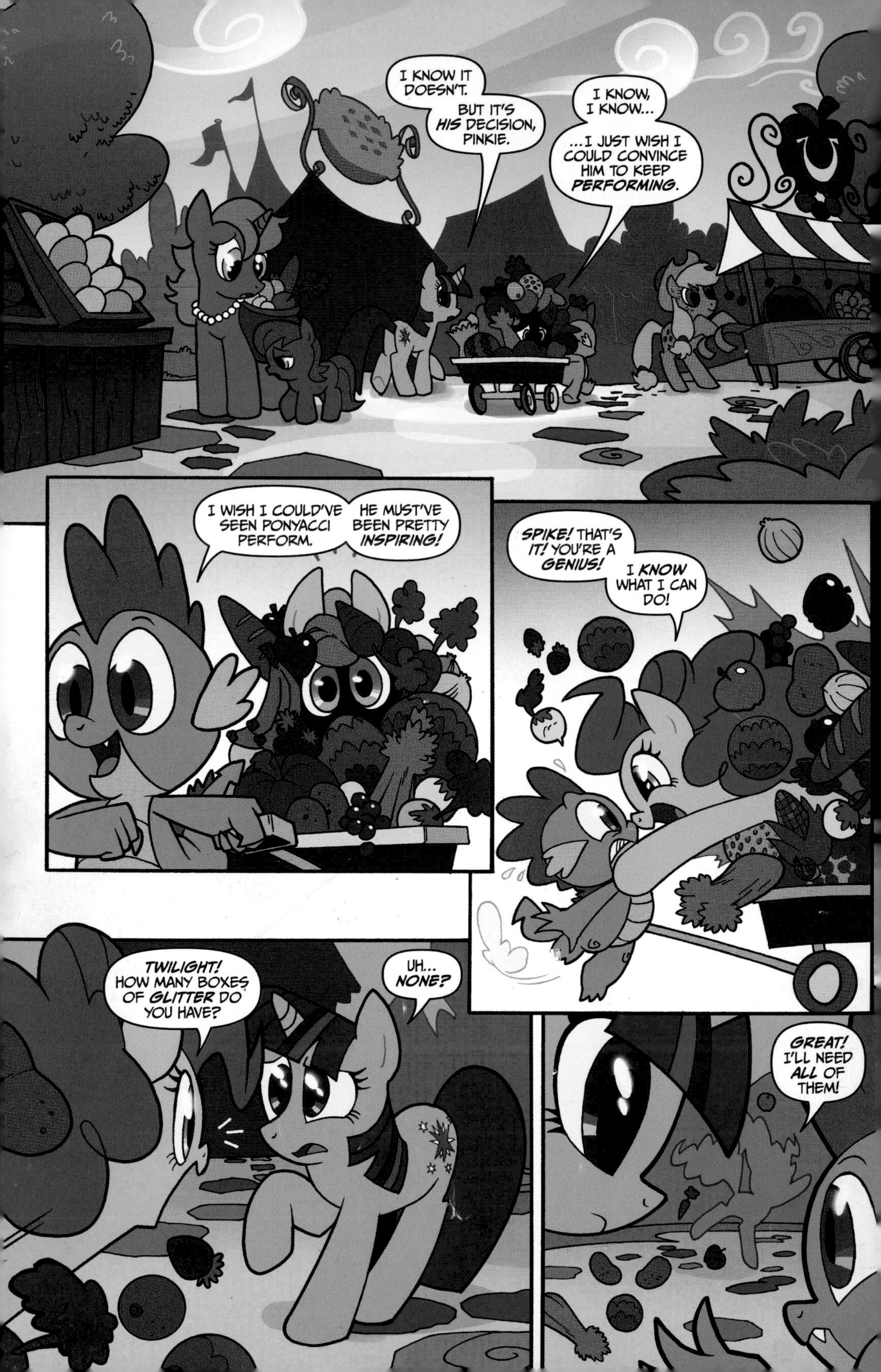
I KNOW IT DOESN'T.
BUT IT'S HIS DECISION, PINKIE.
I KNOW, I KNOW...
...I JUST WISH I COULD CONVINCE HIM TO KEEP PERFORMING.
I WISH I COULD'VE SEEN PONYACCI PERFORM.
HE MUST'VE BEEN PRETTY INSPIRING!
SPIKE! THAT'S IT! YOU'RE A GENIUS!
I KNOW WHAT I CAN DO!
TWILIGHT! HOW MANY BOXES OF GLITTER DO YOU HAVE?
UH... NONE?
GREAT! I'LL NEED ALL OF THEM!

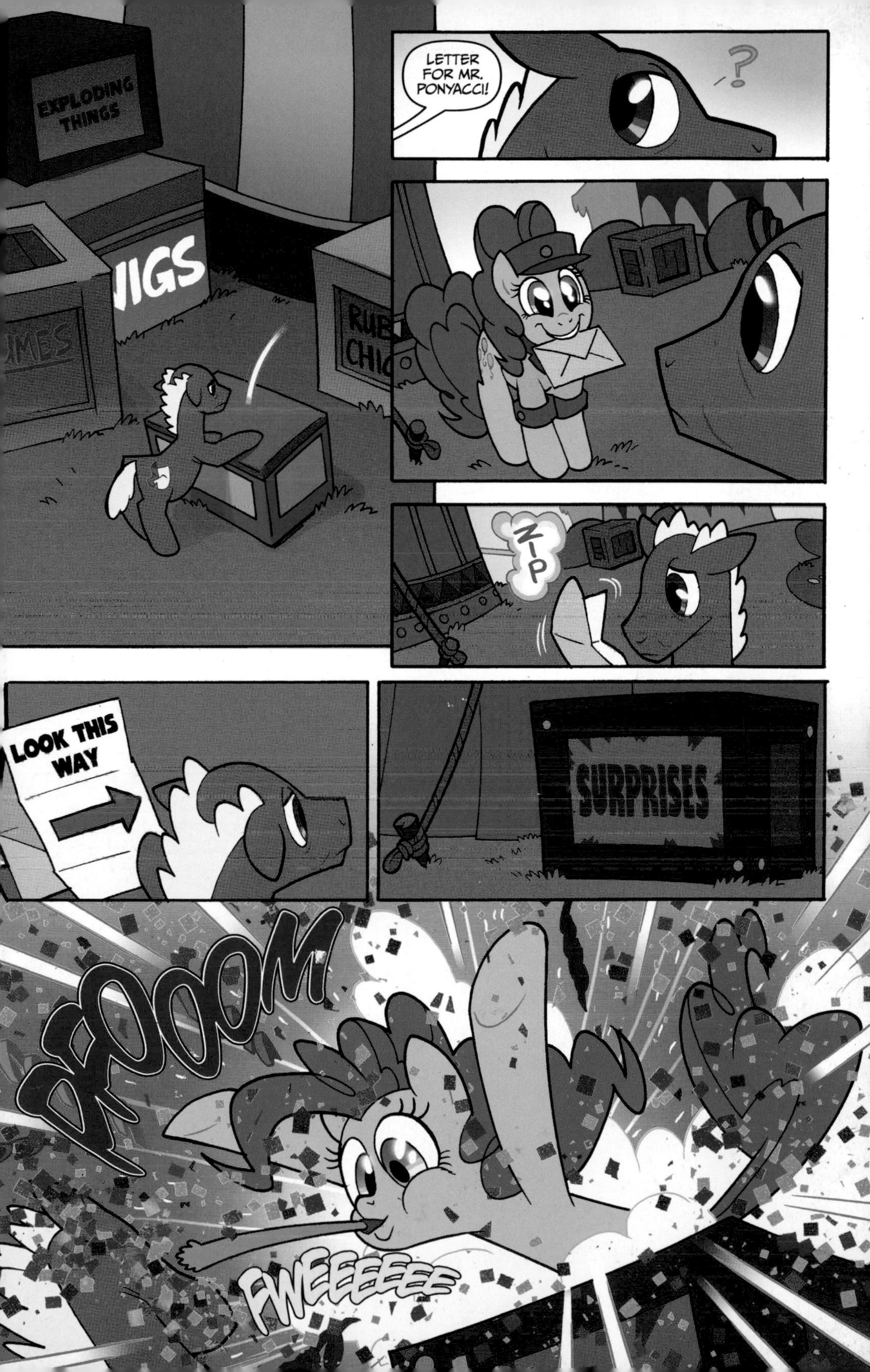
EXPLODING THINGS
WIGS
RUB CHIC
LETTER FOR MR. PONYACCI!
?
ZIP
LOOK THIS WAY
SURPRISES
BOOOOM
FWEEEEEEE

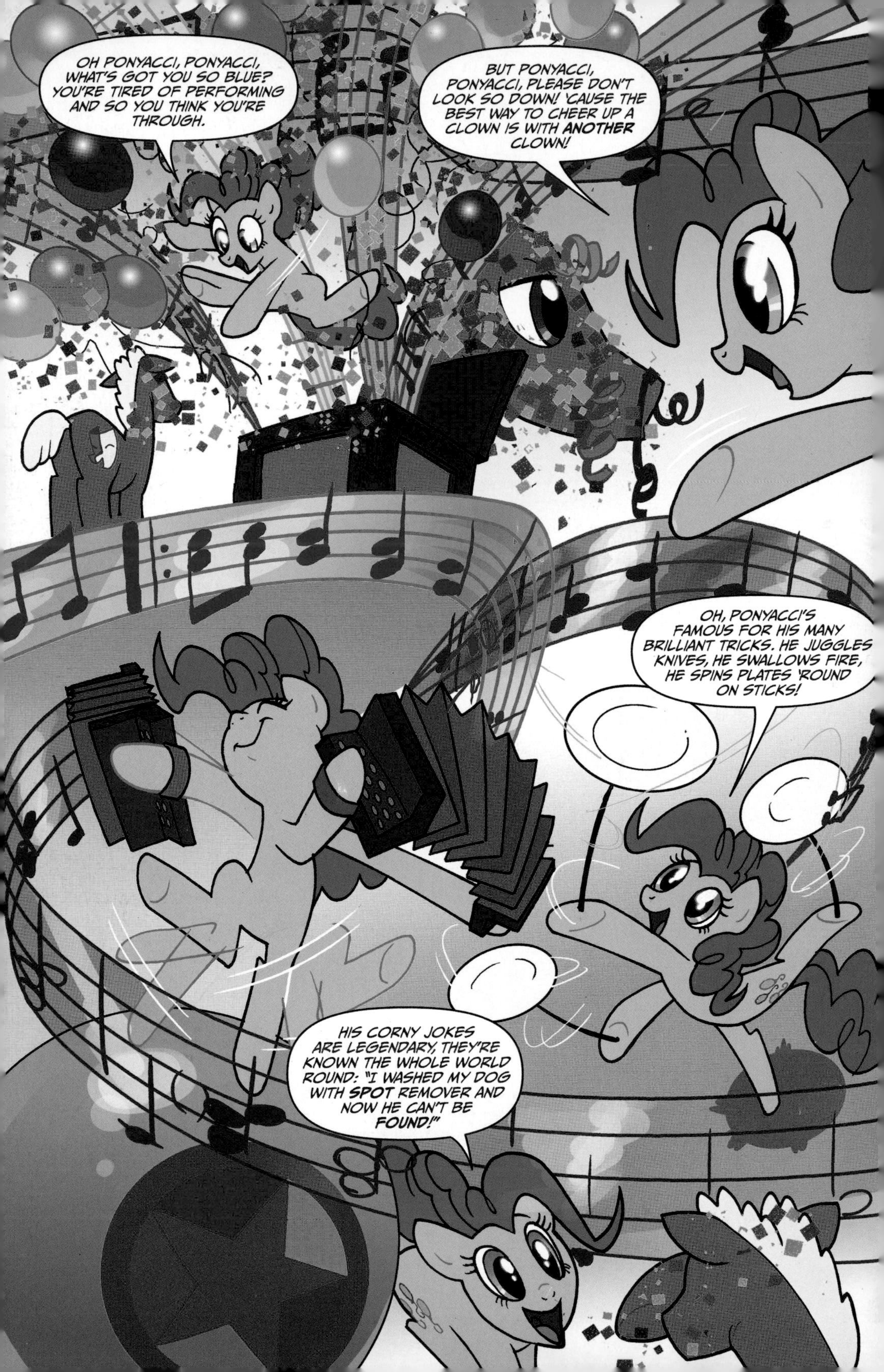
OH PONYACCI, PONYACCI, WHAT'S GOT YOU SO BLUE? YOU'RE TIRED OF PERFORMING AND SO YOU THINK YOU'RE THROUGH.
BUT PONYACCI, PONYACCI, PLEASE DON'T LOOK SO DOWN! 'CAUSE THE BEST WAY TO CHEER UP A CLOWN IS WITH ANOTHER CLOWN!
OH, PONYACCI'S FAMOUS FOR HIS MANY BRILLIANT TRICKS. HE JUGGLES KNIVES, HE SWALLOWS FIRE, HE SPINS PLATES 'ROUND ON STICKS!
HIS CORNY JOKES ARE LEGENDARY, THEY'RE KNOWN THE WHOLE WORLD ROUND: "I WASHED MY DOG WITH SPOT REMOVER AND NOW HE CAN'T BE FOUND!"

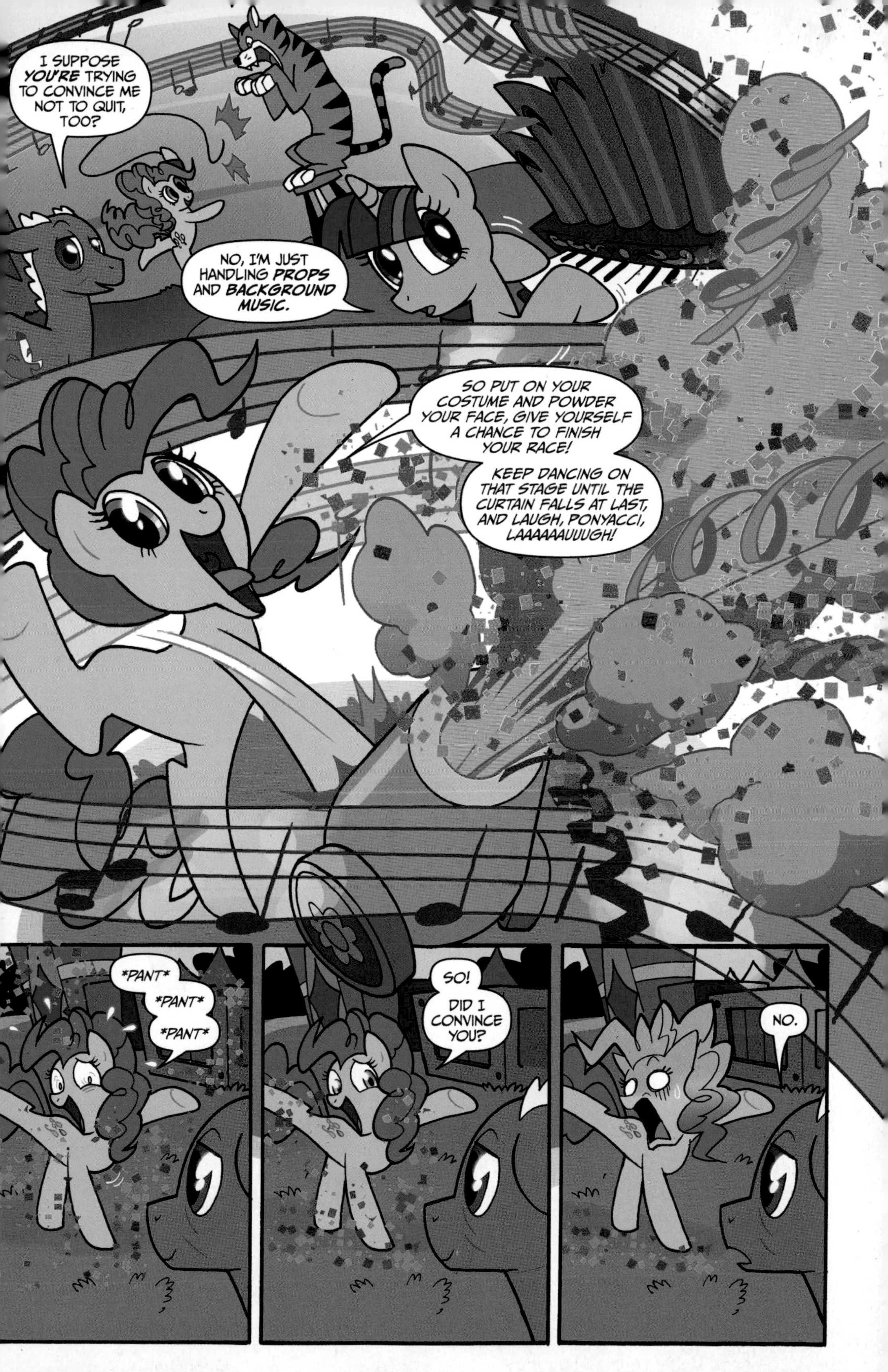
I SUPPOSE YOU'RE TRYING TO CONVINCE ME NOT TO QUIT, TOO?
NO, I'M JUST HANDLING PROPS AND BACKGROUND MUSIC.
SO PUT ON YOUR COSTUME AND POWDER YOUR FACE, GIVE YOURSELF A CHANCE TO FINISH YOUR RACE!
KEEP DANCING ON THAT STAGE UNTIL THE CURTAIN FALLS AT LAST, AND LAUGH, PONYACCI, LAAAAAAUUUGH!
PANT
PANT
PANT
SO!
DID I CONVINCE YOU?
NO.

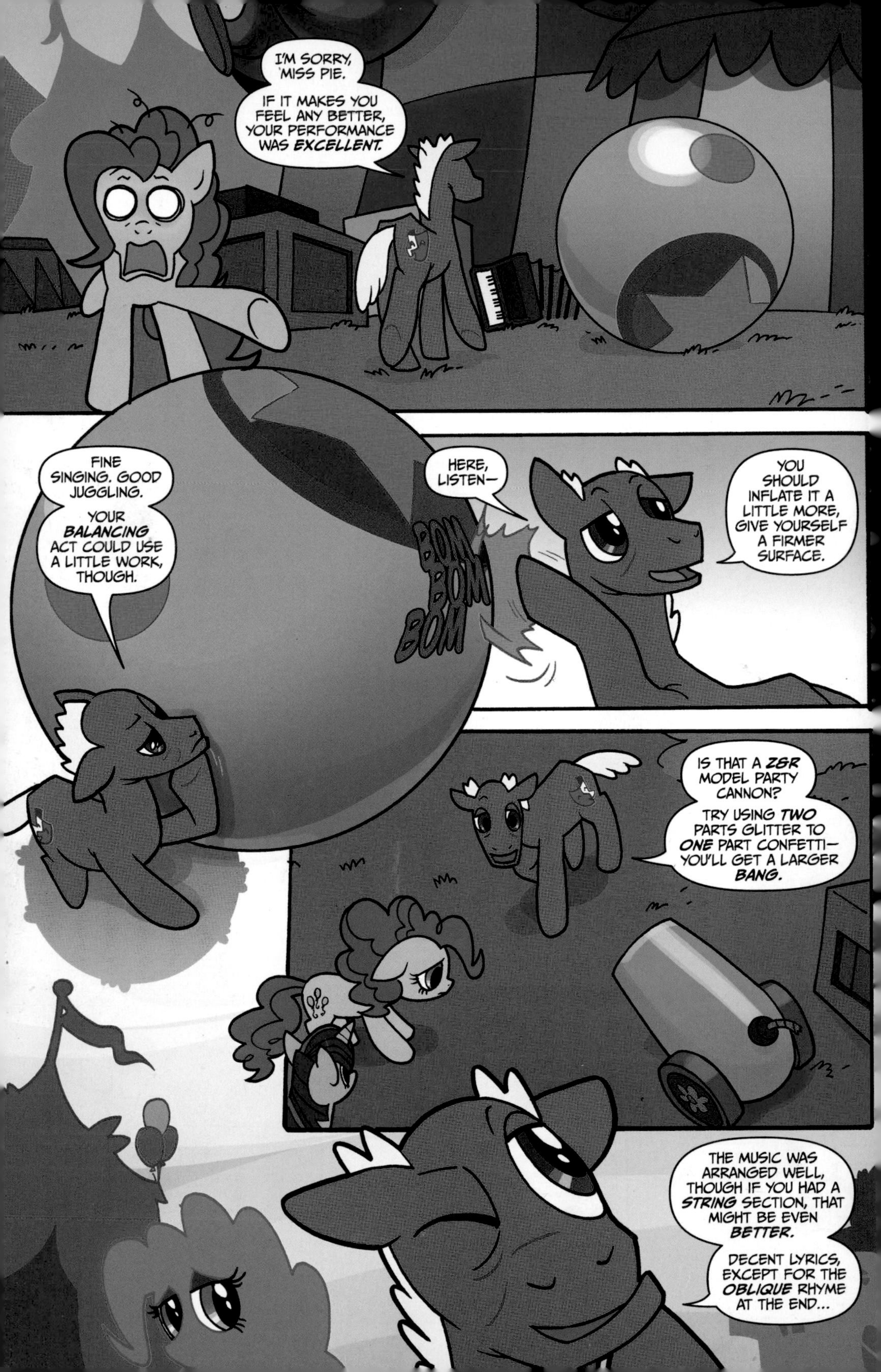
I'M SORRY, MISS PIE.
IF IT MAKES YOU FEEL ANY BETTER, YOUR PERFORMANCE WAS EXCELLENT.
FINE SINGING. GOOD JUGGLING.
YOUR BALANCING ACT COULD USE A LITTLE WORK, THOUGH.
HERE, LISTEN—
BOM BOM BOM
YOU SHOULD INFLATE IT A LITTLE MORE, GIVE YOURSELF A FIRMER SURFACE.
IS THAT A Z&R MODEL PARTY CANNON?
TRY USING TWO PARTS GLITTER TO ONE PART CONFETTI— YOU'LL GET A LARGER BANG.
THE MUSIC WAS ARRANGED WELL, THOUGH IF YOU HAD A STRING SECTION, THAT MIGHT BE EVEN BETTER.
DECENT LYRICS, EXCEPT FOR THE OBLIQUE RHYME AT THE END...

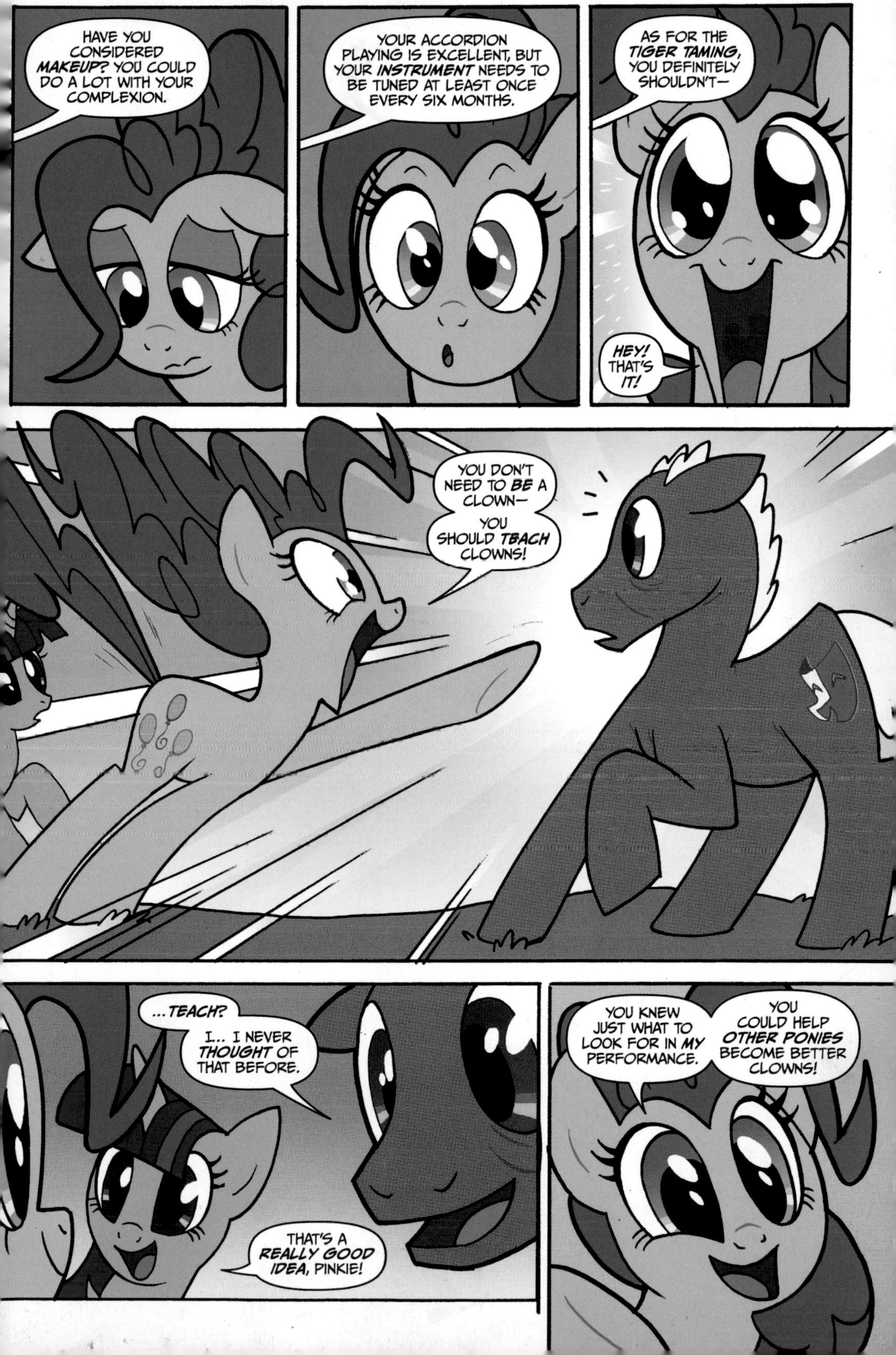
HAVE YOU CONSIDERED MAKEUP? YOU COULD DO A LOT WITH YOUR COMPLEXION.
YOUR ACCORDION PLAYING IS EXCELLENT, BUT YOUR INSTRUMENT NEEDS TO BE TUNED AT LEAST ONCE EVERY SIX MONTHS.
AS FOR THE TIGER TAMING, YOU DEFINITELY SHOULDN'T—
HEY! THAT'S IT!
YOU DON'T NEED TO BE A CLOWN—
YOU SHOULD TEACH CLOWNS!
...TEACH?
I... I NEVER THOUGHT OF THAT BEFORE.
THAT'S A REALLY GOOD IDEA, PINKIE!
YOU KNEW JUST WHAT TO LOOK FOR IN MY PERFORMANCE.
YOU COULD HELP OTHER PONIES BECOME BETTER CLOWNS!

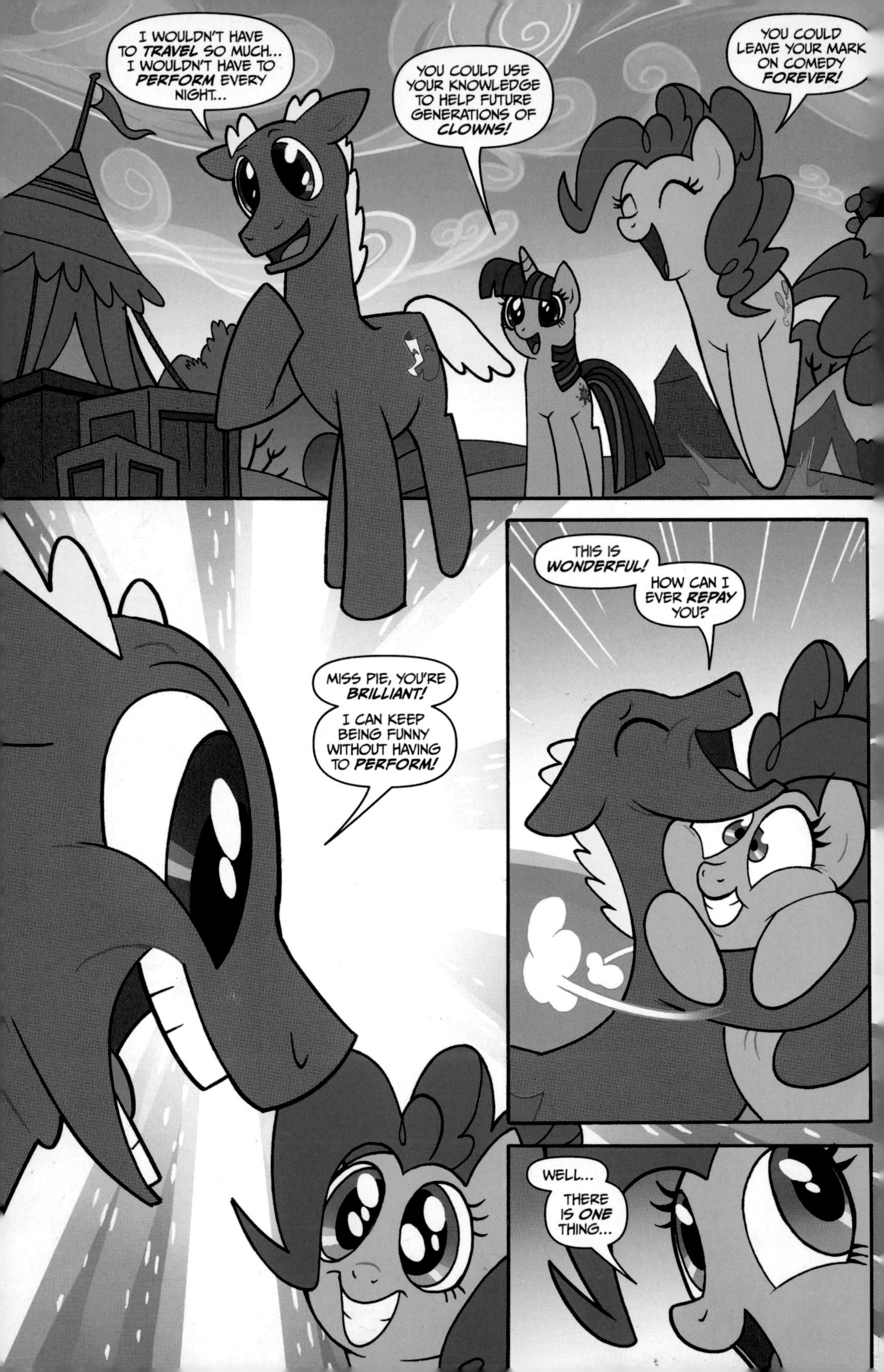
I WOULDN'T HAVE TO TRAVEL SO MUCH... I WOULDN'T HAVE TO PERFORM EVERY NIGHT...
YOU COULD USE YOUR KNOWLEDGE TO HELP FUTURE GENERATIONS OF CLOWNS!
YOU COULD LEAVE YOUR MARK ON COMEDY FOREVER!
MISS PIE, YOU'RE BRILLIANT!
I CAN KEEP BEING FUNNY WITHOUT HAVING TO PERFORM!
THIS IS WONDERFUL!
HOW CAN I EVER REPAY YOU?
WELL...
THERE IS ONE THING...

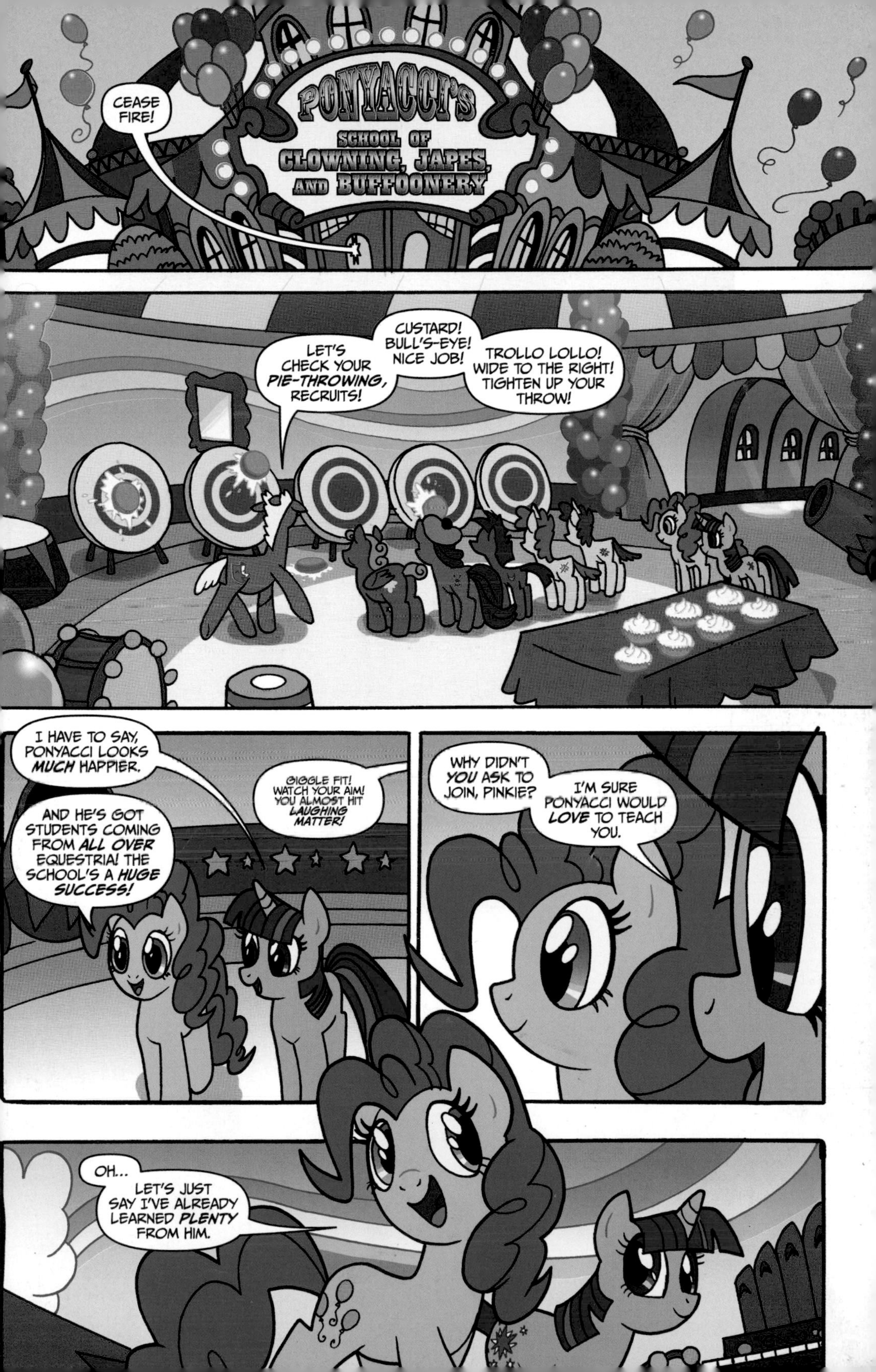

PONYACCI'S
SCHOOL OF CLOWNING, JAPES, AND BUFFOONERY
CEASE FIRE!
LET'S CHECK YOUR PIE-THROWING, RECRUITS!
CUSTARD! BULL'S-EYE! NICE JOB!
TROLLO LOLLO! WIDE TO THE RIGHT! TIGHTEN UP YOUR THROW!
I HAVE TO SAY, PONYACCI LOOKS MUCH HAPPIER.
AND HE'S GOT STUDENTS COMING FROM ALL OVER EQUESTRIA! THE SCHOOL'S A HUGE SUCCESS!
GIGGLE FIT! WATCH YOUR AIM! YOU ALMOST HIT LAUGHING MATTER!
WHY DIDN'T YOU ASK TO JOIN, PINKIE?
I'M SURE PONYACCI WOULD LOVE TO TEACH YOU.
OH...
LET'S JUST SAY I'VE ALREADY LEARNED PLENTY FROM HIM.

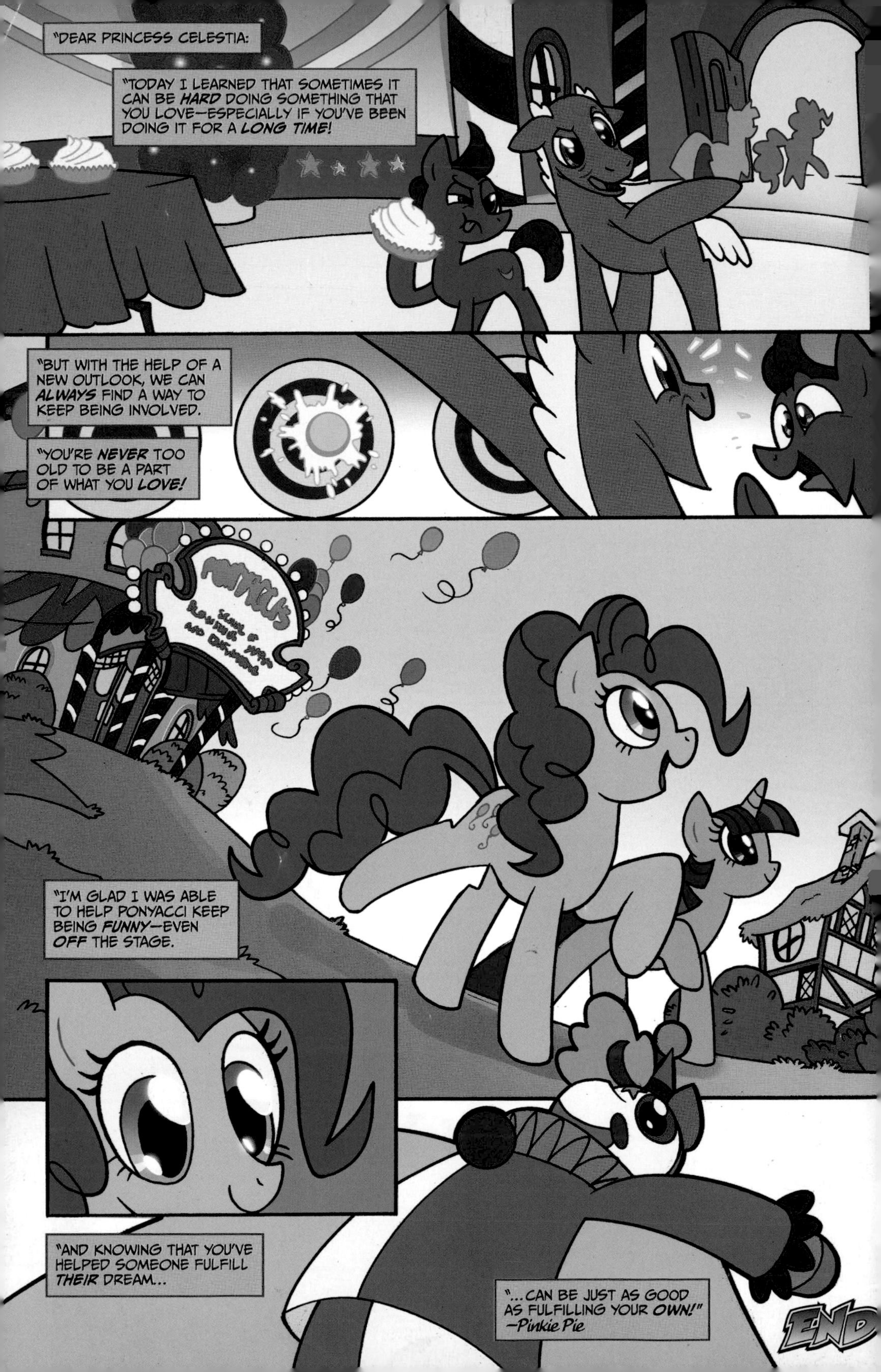
"DEAR PRINCESS CELESTIA:
"TODAY I LEARNED THAT SOMETIMES IT CAN BE HARD DOING SOMETHING THAT YOU LOVE—ESPECIALLY IF YOU'VE BEEN DOING IT FOR A LONG TIME!
"BUT WITH THE HELP OF A NEW OUTLOOK, WE CAN ALWAYS FIND A WAY TO KEEP BEING INVOLVED.
"YOU'RE NEVER TOO OLD TO BE A PART OF WHAT YOU LOVE!
"I'M GLAD I WAS ABLE TO HELP PONYACCI KEEP BEING FUNNY—EVEN OFF THE STAGE.
"AND KNOWING THAT YOU'VE HELPED SOMEONE FULFILL THEIR DREAM...
"...CAN BE JUST AS GOOD AS FULFILLING YOUR OWN!" —Pinkie Pie
END

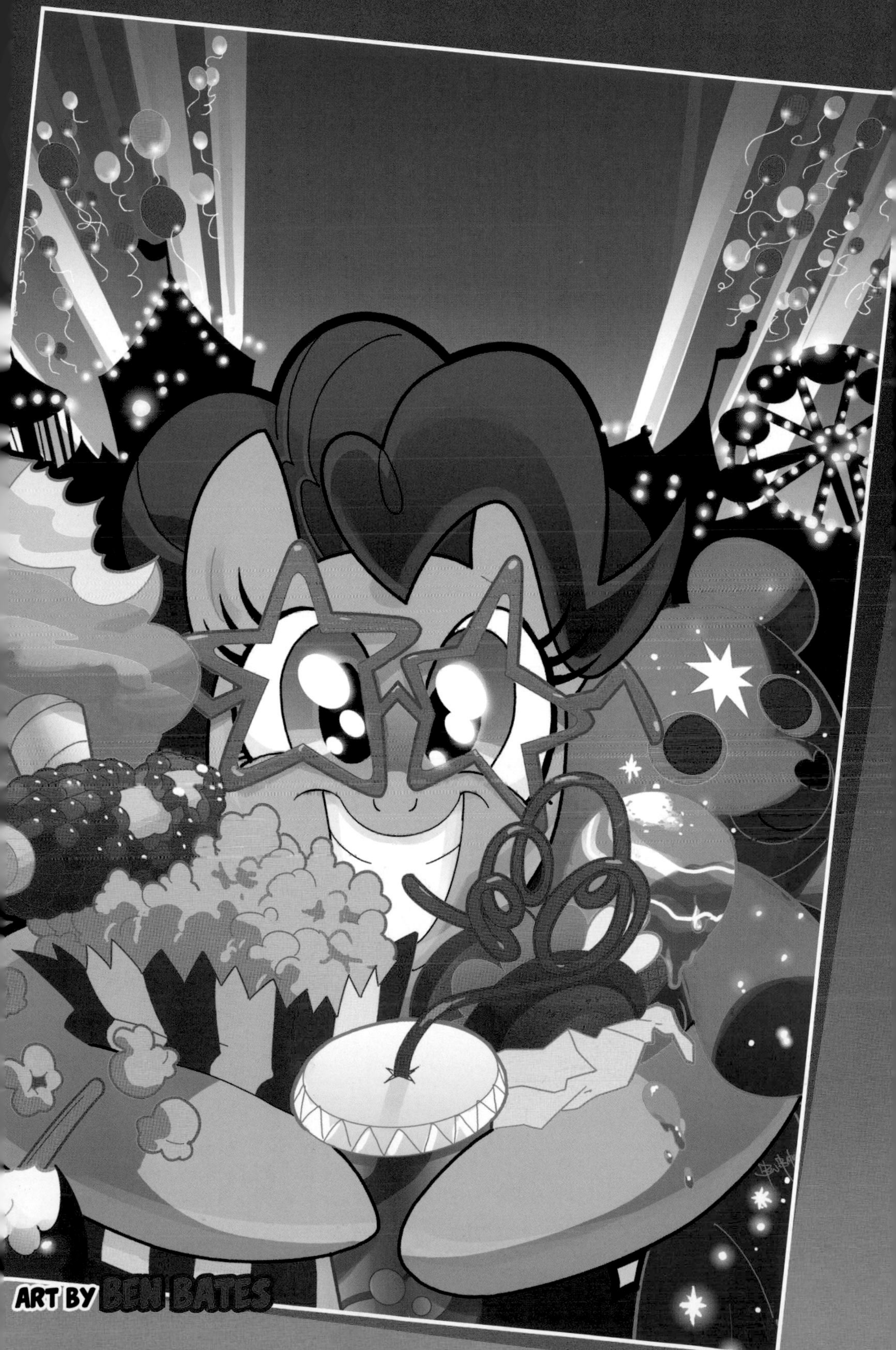
ART BY BEN BATES

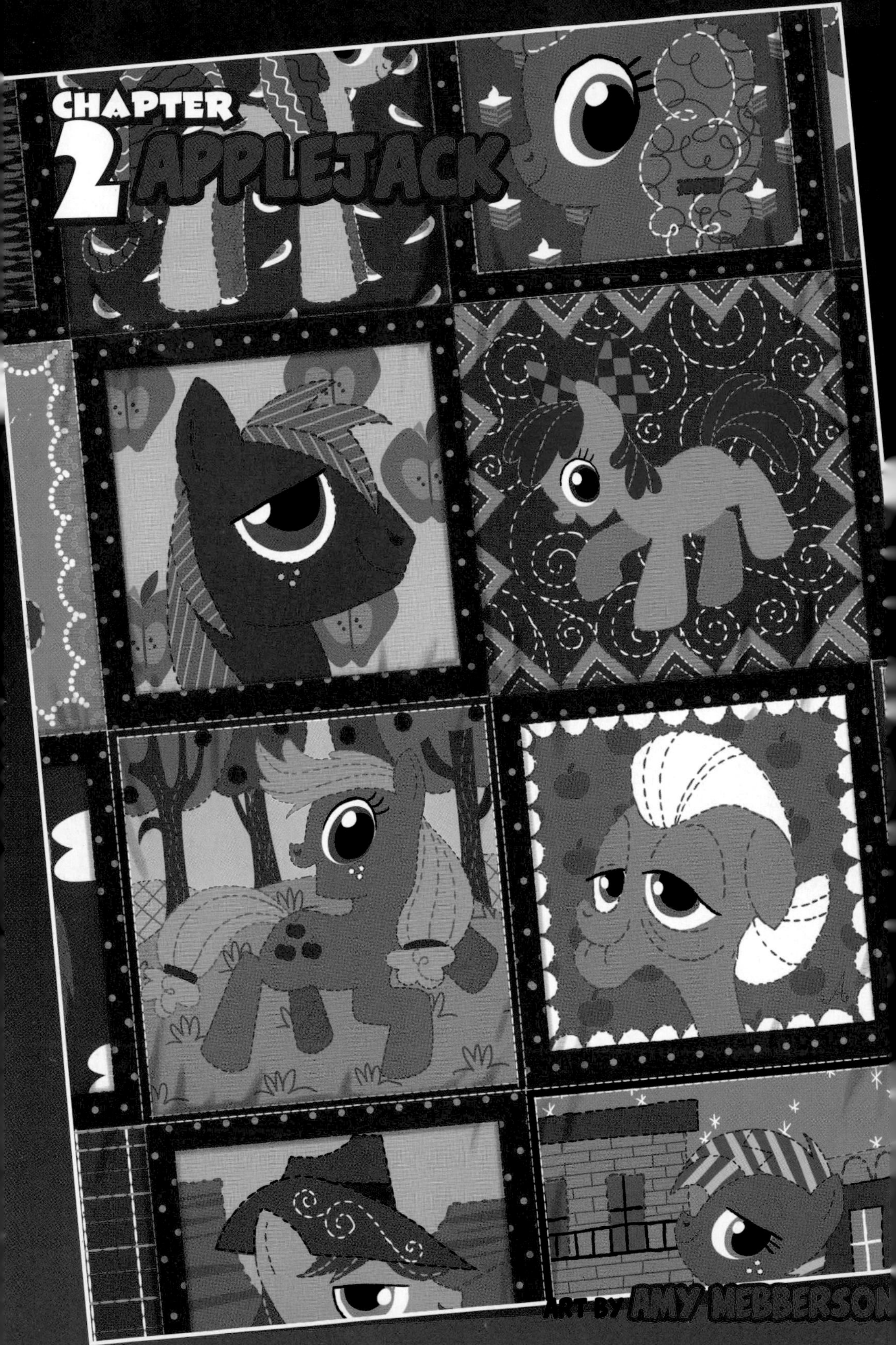
CHAPTER 2 APPLEJACK
ART BY AMY MEBBERSON

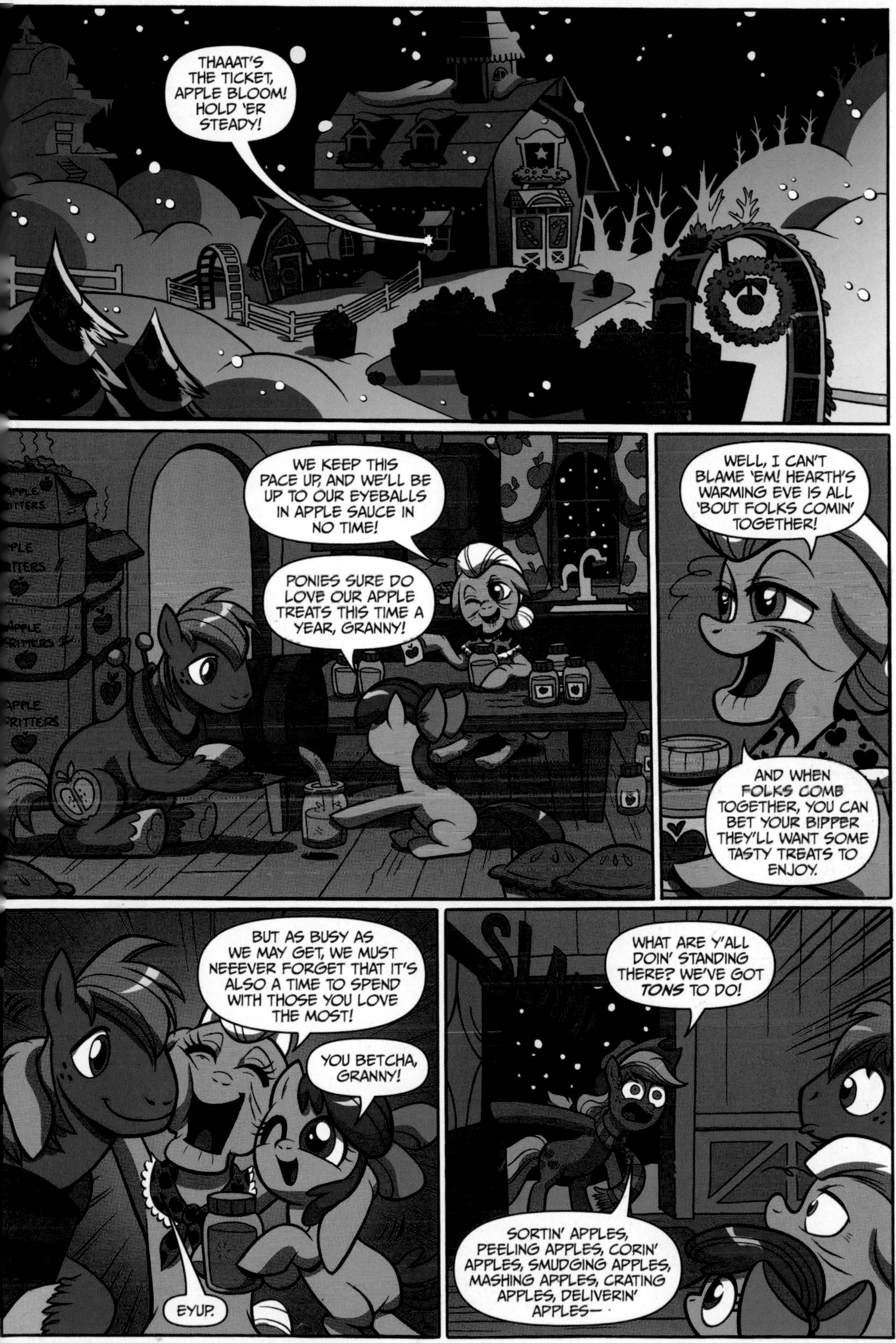
THAAAT'S THE TICKET, APPLE BLOOM! HOLD 'ER STEADY!
WE KEEP THIS PACE UP, AND WE'LL BE UP TO OUR EYEBALLS IN APPLE SAUCE IN NO TIME!
PONIES SURE DO LOVE OUR APPLE TREATS THIS TIME A YEAR, GRANNY!
WELL, I CAN'T BLAME 'EM! HEARTH'S WARMING EVE IS ALL 'BOUT FOLKS COMIN' TOGETHER!
AND WHEN FOLKS COME TOGETHER, YOU CAN BET YOUR BIPPER THEY'LL WANT SOME TASTY TREATS TO ENJOY.
BUT AS BUSY AS WE MAY GET, WE MUST NEEEVER FORGET THAT IT'S ALSO A TIME TO SPEND WITH THOSE YOU LOVE THE MOST!
YOU BETCHA, GRANNY!
EYUP.
WHAT ARE Y'ALL DOIN' STANDING THERE? WE'VE GOT TONS TO DO!
SORTIN' APPLES, PEELING APPLES, CORIN' APPLES, SMUDGING APPLES, MASHING APPLES, CRATING APPLES, DELIVERIN' APPLES—

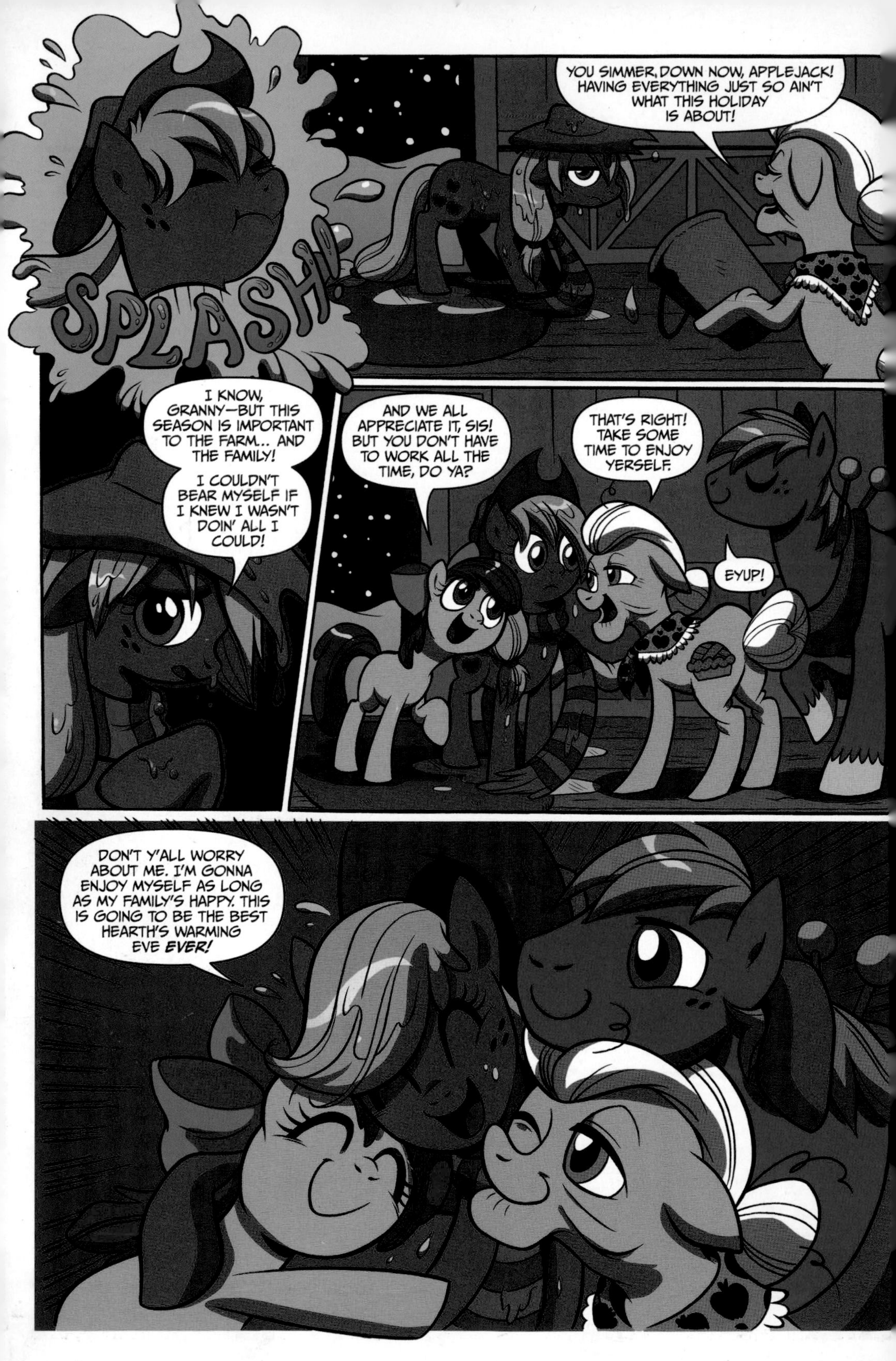
SPLASH!
YOU SIMMER DOWN NOW, APPLEJACK! HAVING EVERYTHING JUST SO AIN'T WHAT THIS HOLIDAY IS ABOUT!
I KNOW, GRANNY—BUT THIS SEASON IS IMPORTANT TO THE FARM... AND THE FAMILY!
I COULDN'T BEAR MYSELF IF I KNEW I WASN'T DOIN' ALL I COULD!
AND WE ALL APPRECIATE IT, SIS! BUT YOU DON'T HAVE TO WORK ALL THE TIME, DO YA?
THAT'S RIGHT! TAKE SOME TIME TO ENJOY YERSELF.
EYUP!
DON'T Y'ALL WORRY ABOUT ME. I'M GONNA ENJOY MYSELF AS LONG AS MY FAMILY'S HAPPY. THIS IS GOING TO BE THE BEST HEARTH'S WARMING EVE *EVER!*

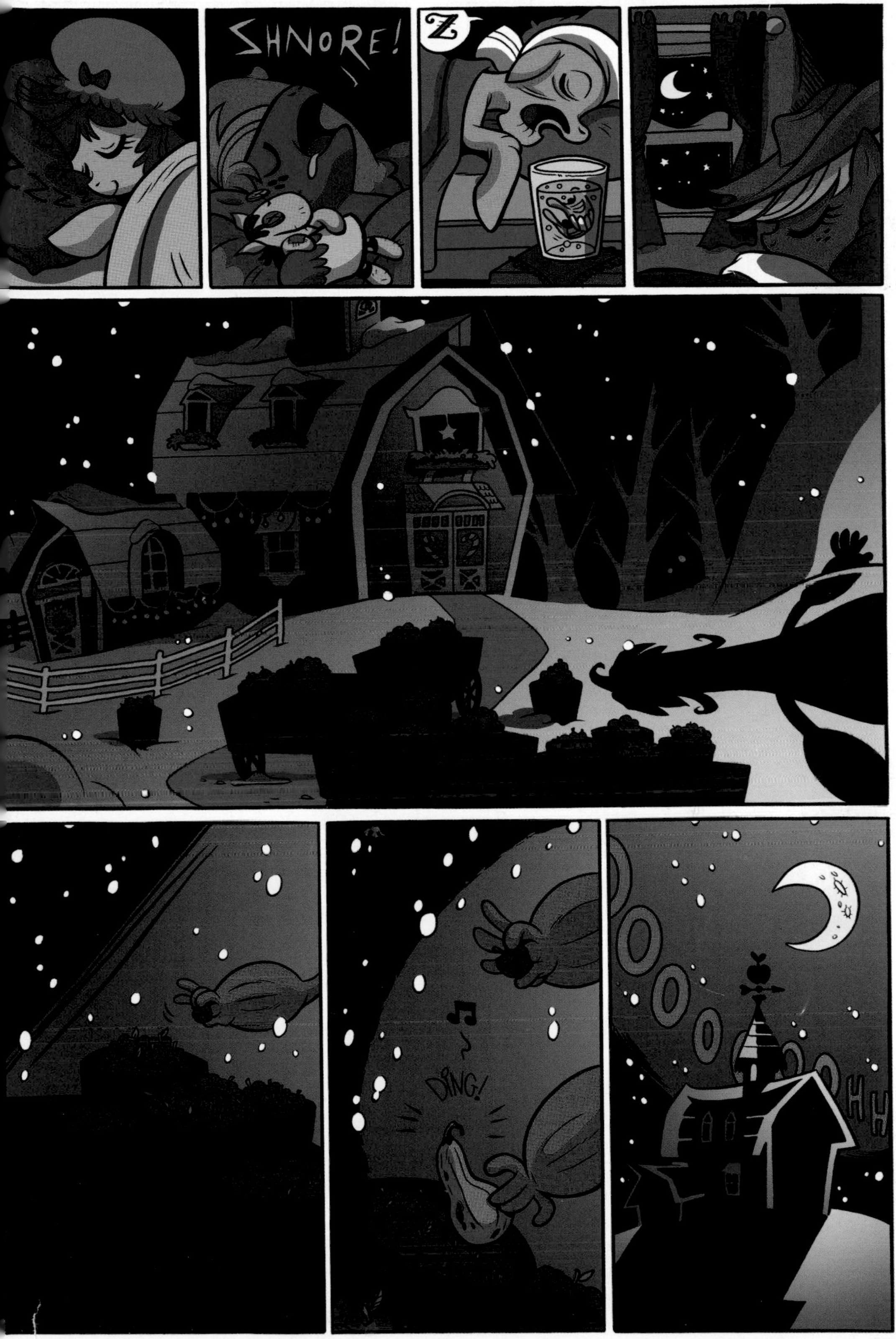
SHNORE!
Z
DING!
OOOOOOHH

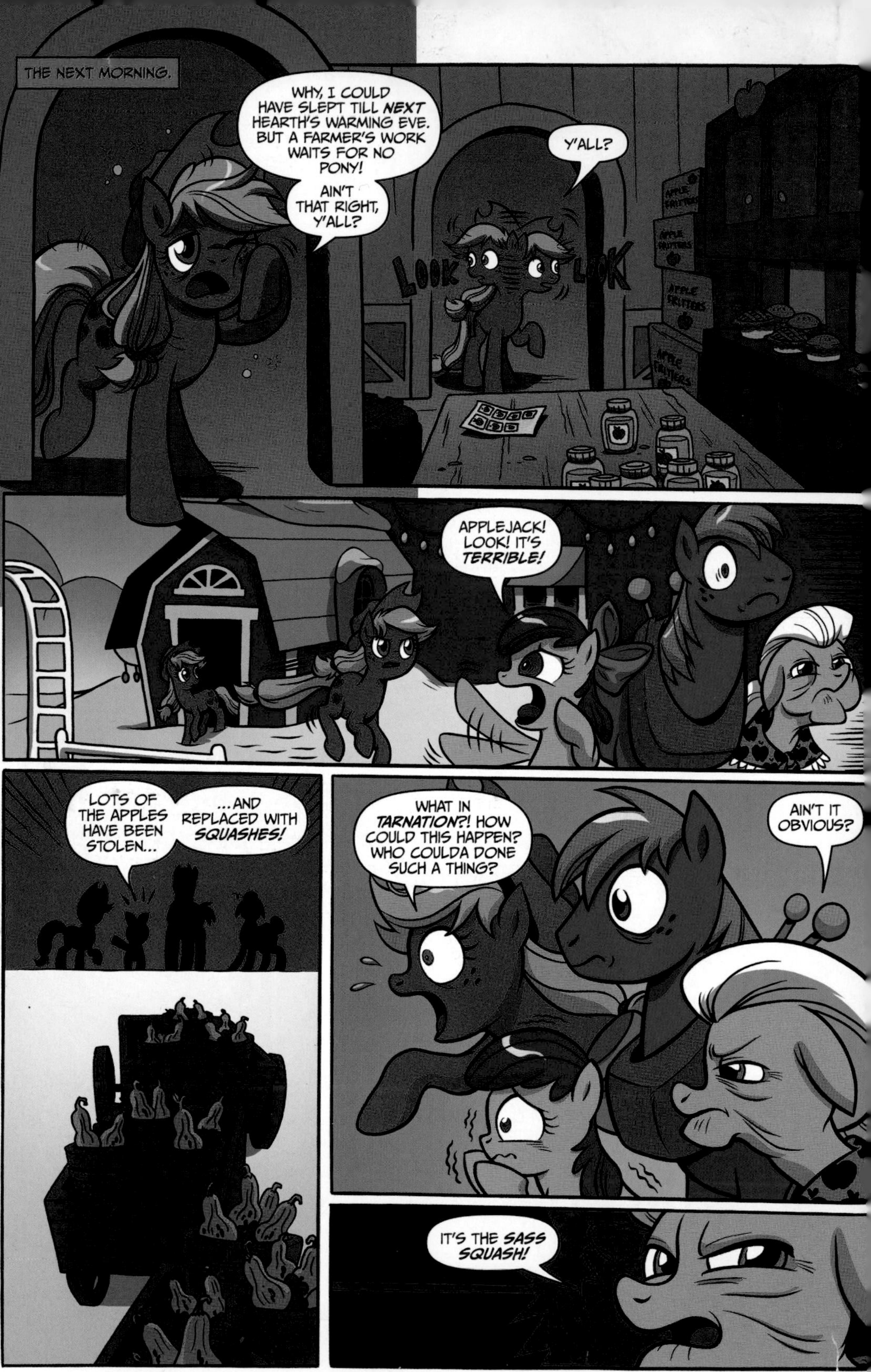
THE NEXT MORNING.
WHY, I COULD HAVE SLEPT TILL NEXT HEARTH'S WARMING EVE. BUT A FARMER'S WORK WAITS FOR NO PONY!
AIN'T THAT RIGHT, Y'ALL?
Y'ALL?
LOOK
LOOK
APPLE FRITTERS
APPLE FRITTERS
APPLE FRITTERS
APPLE FRITTERS
APPLEJACK! LOOK! IT'S TERRIBLE!
LOTS OF THE APPLES HAVE BEEN STOLEN...
...AND REPLACED WITH SQUASHES!
WHAT IN TARNATION?! HOW COULD THIS HAPPEN? WHO COULDA DONE SUCH A THING?
AIN'T IT OBVIOUS?
IT'S THE SASS SQUASH!

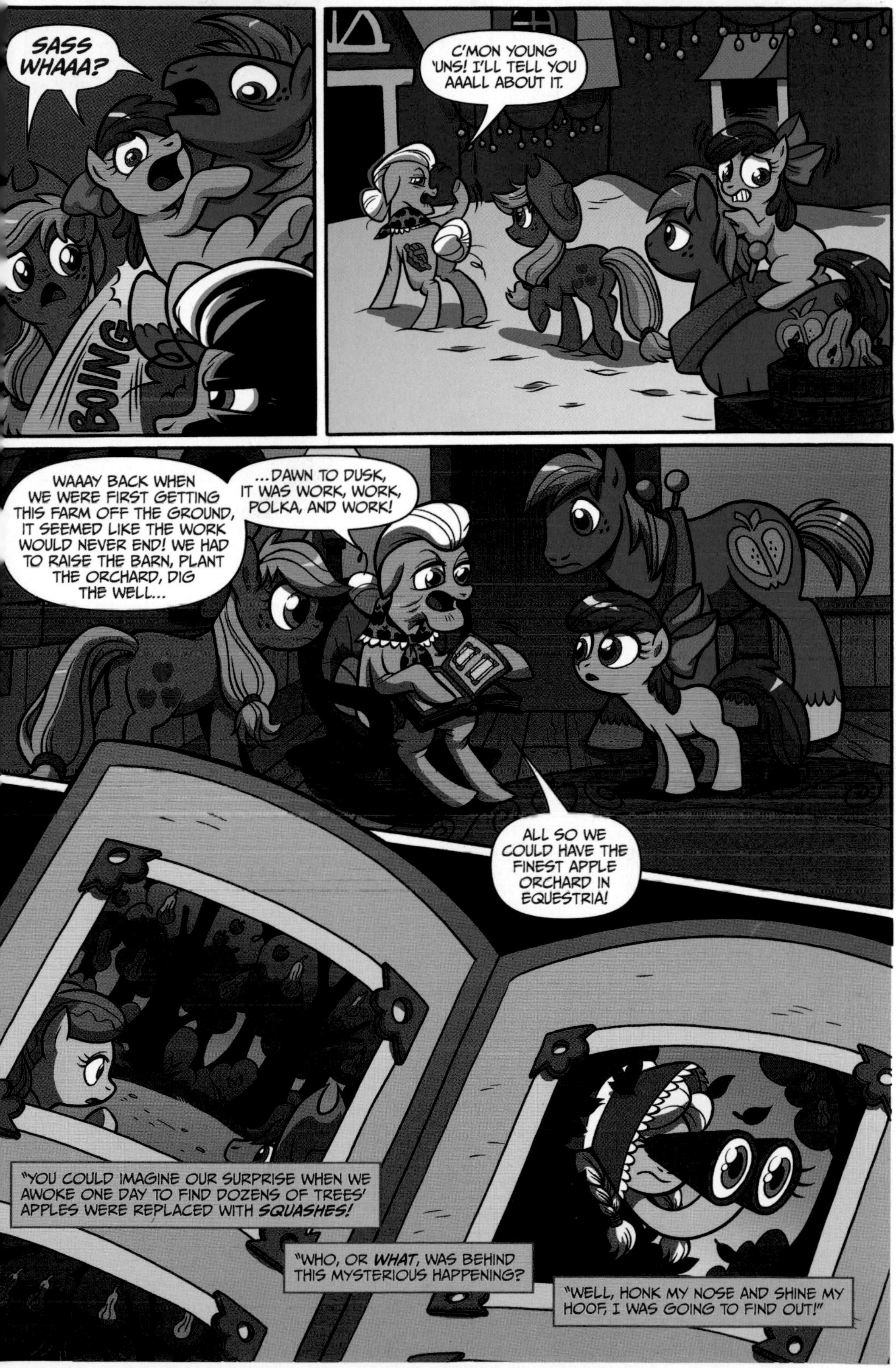
SASS WHAAA?
BOING
C'MON YOUNG 'UNS! I'LL TELL YOU AAALL ABOUT IT.
WAAAY BACK WHEN WE WERE FIRST GETTING THIS FARM OFF THE GROUND, IT SEEMED LIKE THE WORK WOULD NEVER END! WE HAD TO RAISE THE BARN, PLANT THE ORCHARD, DIG THE WELL...
...DAWN TO DUSK, IT WAS WORK, WORK, POLKA, AND WORK!
ALL SO WE COULD HAVE THE FINEST APPLE ORCHARD IN EQUESTRIA!
"YOU COULD IMAGINE OUR SURPRISE WHEN WE AWOKE ONE DAY TO FIND DOZENS OF TREES' APPLES WERE REPLACED WITH SQUASHES!
"WHO, OR WHAT, WAS BEHIND THIS MYSTERIOUS HAPPENING?
"WELL, HONK MY NOSE AND SHINE MY HOOF, I WAS GOING TO FIND OUT!"

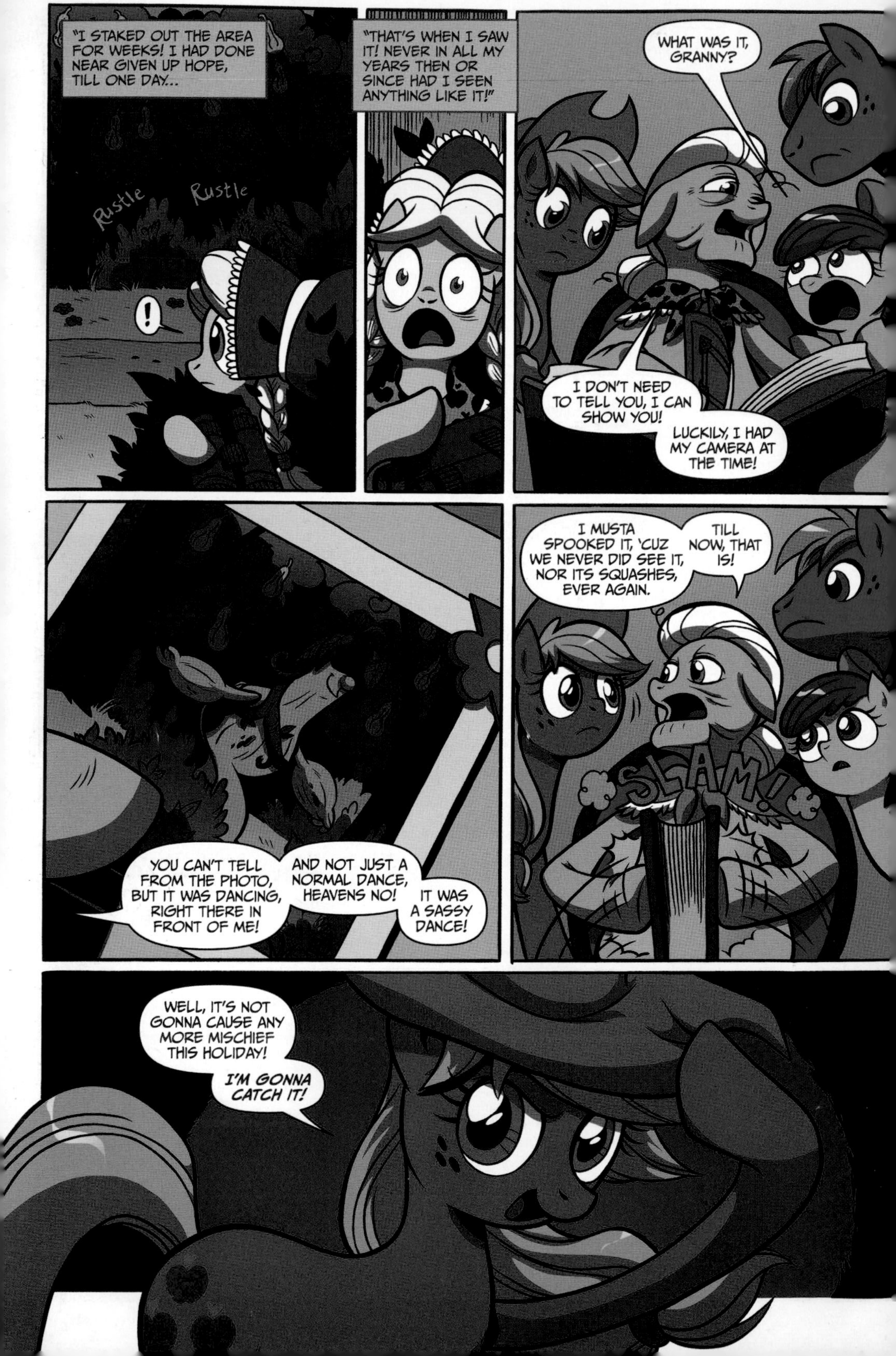
"I STAKED OUT THE AREA FOR WEEKS! I HAD DONE NEAR GIVEN UP HOPE, TILL ONE DAY...
Rustle Rustle
!
"THAT'S WHEN I SAW IT! NEVER IN ALL MY YEARS THEN OR SINCE HAD I SEEN ANYTHING LIKE IT!"
WHAT WAS IT, GRANNY?
I DON'T NEED TO TELL YOU, I CAN SHOW YOU!
LUCKILY, I HAD MY CAMERA AT THE TIME!
YOU CAN'T TELL FROM THE PHOTO, BUT IT WAS DANCING, RIGHT THERE IN FRONT OF ME!
AND NOT JUST A NORMAL DANCE, HEAVENS NO!
IT WAS A SASSY DANCE!
I MUSTA SPOOKED IT, 'CUZ WE NEVER DID SEE IT, NOR ITS SQUASHES, EVER AGAIN.
TILL NOW, THAT IS!
SLAM!
WELL, IT'S NOT GONNA CAUSE ANY MORE MISCHIEF THIS HOLIDAY!
I'M GONNA CATCH IT!

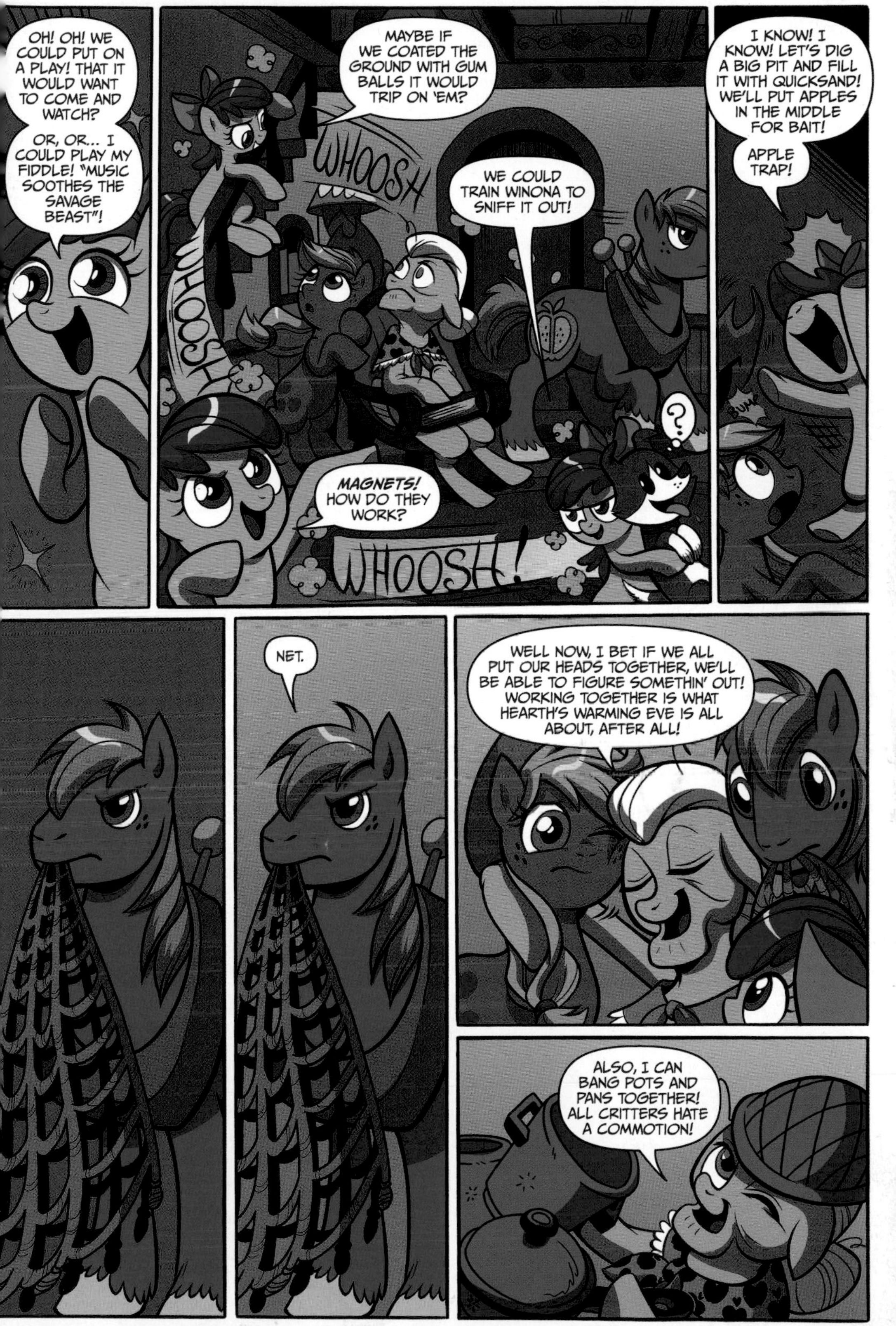
OH! OH! WE COULD PUT ON A PLAY! THAT IT WOULD WANT TO COME AND WATCH?
OR, OR... I COULD PLAY MY FIDDLE! "MUSIC SOOTHES THE SAVAGE BEAST"!
MAYBE IF WE COATED THE GROUND WITH GUM BALLS IT WOULD TRIP ON 'EM?
WHOOSH
WHOOSH
WE COULD TRAIN WINONA TO SNIFF IT OUT!
MAGNETS! HOW DO THEY WORK?
?
WHOOSH!
I KNOW! I KNOW! LET'S DIG A BIG PIT AND FILL IT WITH QUICKSAND! WE'LL PUT APPLES IN THE MIDDLE FOR BAIT!
APPLE TRAP!
NET.
WELL NOW, I BET IF WE ALL PUT OUR HEADS TOGETHER, WE'LL BE ABLE TO FIGURE SOMETHIN' OUT! WORKING TOGETHER IS WHAT HEARTH'S WARMING EVE IS ALL ABOUT, AFTER ALL!
ALSO, I CAN BANG POTS AND PANS TOGETHER! ALL CRITTERS HATE A COMMOTION!

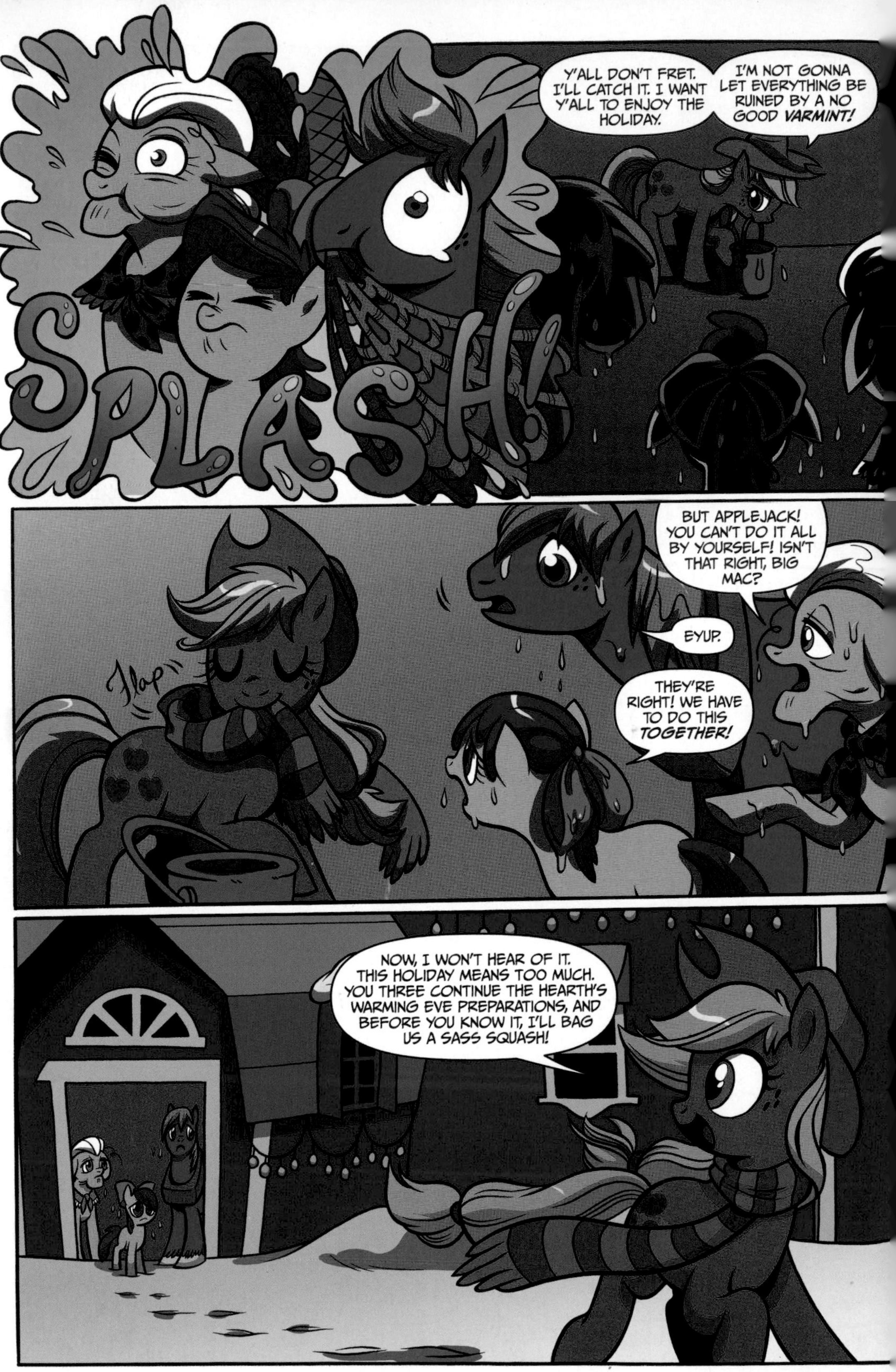
SPLASH!
Y'ALL DON'T FRET. I'LL CATCH IT. I WANT Y'ALL TO ENJOY THE HOLIDAY.
I'M NOT GONNA LET EVERYTHING BE RUINED BY A NO GOOD VARMINT!
Flap
BUT APPLEJACK! YOU CAN'T DO IT ALL BY YOURSELF! ISN'T THAT RIGHT, BIG MAC?
EYUP.
THEY'RE RIGHT! WE HAVE TO DO THIS TOGETHER!
NOW, I WON'T HEAR OF IT. THIS HOLIDAY MEANS TOO MUCH. YOU THREE CONTINUE THE HEARTH'S WARMING EVE PREPARATIONS, AND BEFORE YOU KNOW IT, I'LL BAG US A SASS SQUASH!

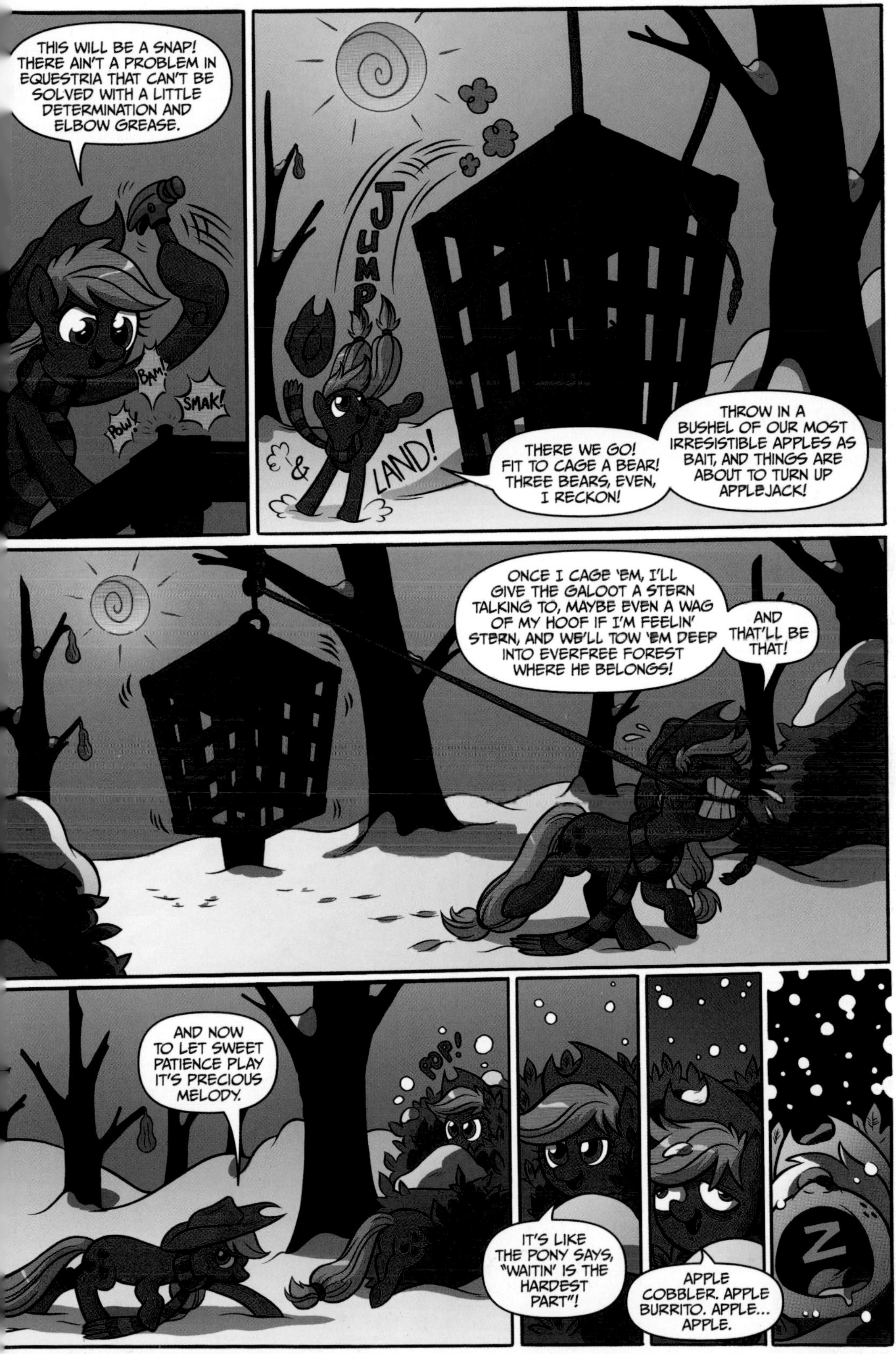
THIS WILL BE A SNAP! THERE AIN'T A PROBLEM IN EQUESTRIA THAT CAN'T BE SOLVED WITH A LITTLE DETERMINATION AND ELBOW GREASE.
BAM!
SMAK!
POW!
JUMP
&
LAND!
THERE WE GO! FIT TO CAGE A BEAR! THREE BEARS, EVEN, I RECKON!
THROW IN A BUSHEL OF OUR MOST IRRESISTIBLE APPLES AS BAIT, AND THINGS ARE ABOUT TO TURN UP APPLEJACK!
ONCE I CAGE 'EM, I'LL GIVE THE GALOOT A STERN TALKING TO, MAYBE EVEN A WAG OF MY HOOF IF I'M FEELIN' STERN, AND WE'LL TOW 'EM DEEP INTO EVERFREE FOREST WHERE HE BELONGS!
AND THAT'LL BE THAT!
AND NOW TO LET SWEET PATIENCE PLAY IT'S PRECIOUS MELODY.
POP!
IT'S LIKE THE PONY SAYS, "WAITIN' IS THE HARDEST PART"!
APPLE COBBLER. APPLE BURRITO. APPLE... APPLE.
Z

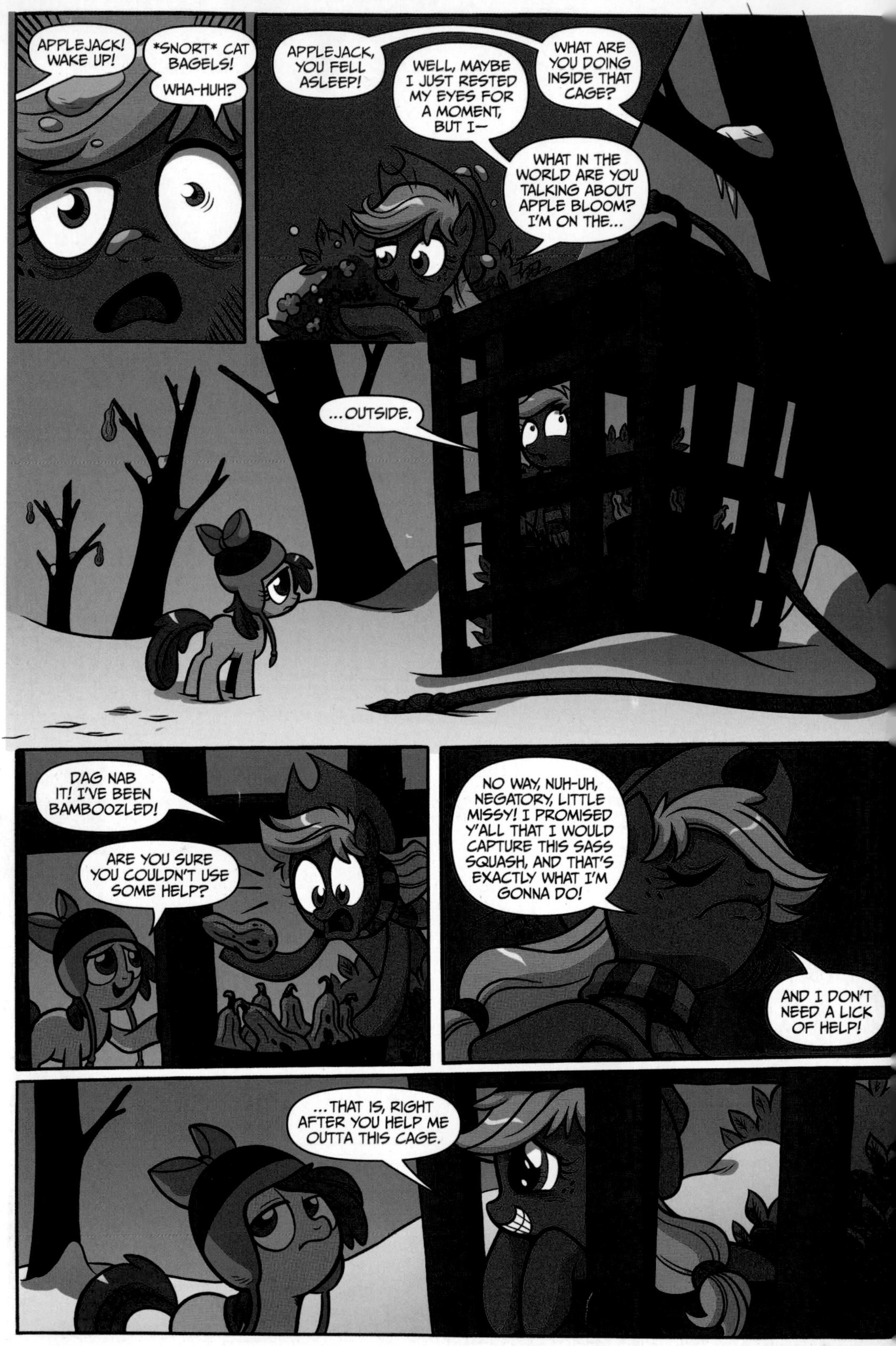
APPLEJACK! WAKE UP!
SNORT CAT BAGELS!
WHA-HUH?
APPLEJACK, YOU FELL ASLEEP!
WELL, MAYBE I JUST RESTED MY EYES FOR A MOMENT, BUT I—
WHAT ARE YOU DOING INSIDE THAT CAGE?
WHAT IN THE WORLD ARE YOU TALKING ABOUT APPLE BLOOM? I'M ON THE...
...OUTSIDE.
DAG NAB IT! I'VE BEEN BAMBOOZLED!
ARE YOU SURE YOU COULDN'T USE SOME HELP?
NO WAY, NUH-UH, NEGATORY, LITTLE MISSY! I PROMISED Y'ALL THAT I WOULD CAPTURE THIS SASS SQUASH, AND THAT'S EXACTLY WHAT I'M GONNA DO!
AND I DON'T NEED A LICK OF HELP!
...THAT IS, RIGHT AFTER YOU HELP ME OUTTA THIS CAGE.

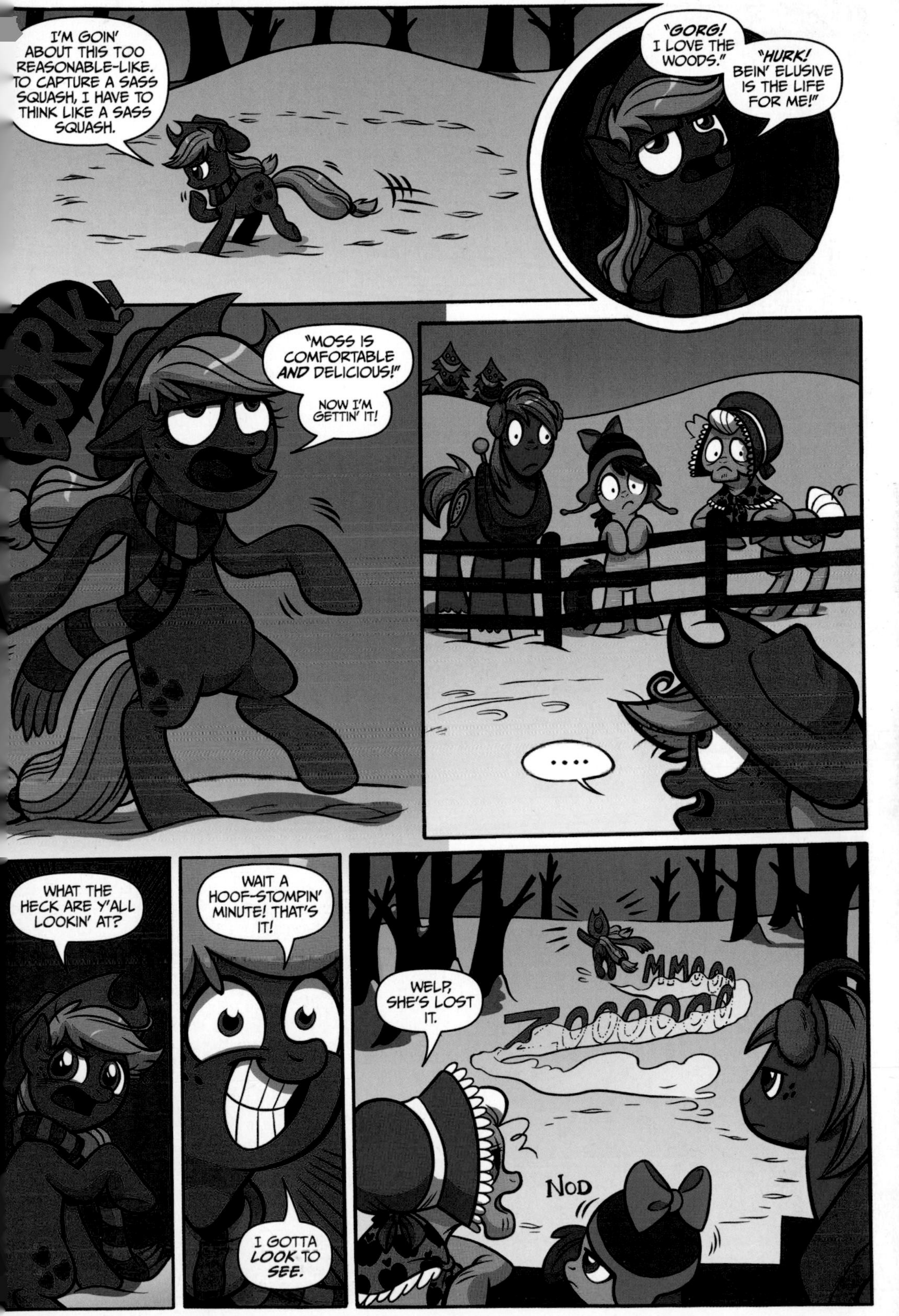
I'M GOIN' ABOUT THIS TOO REASONABLE-LIKE. TO CAPTURE A SASS SQUASH, I HAVE TO THINK LIKE A SASS SQUASH.
"GORG! I LOVE THE WOODS."
"HURK! BEIN' ELUSIVE IS THE LIFE FOR ME!"
BORK!
"MOSS IS COMFORTABLE AND DELICIOUS!"
NOW I'M GETTIN' IT!
....
WHAT THE HECK ARE Y'ALL LOOKIN' AT?
WAIT A HOOF-STOMPIN' MINUTE! THAT'S IT!
I GOTTA LOOK TO SEE.
WELP, SHE'S LOST IT.
NOD

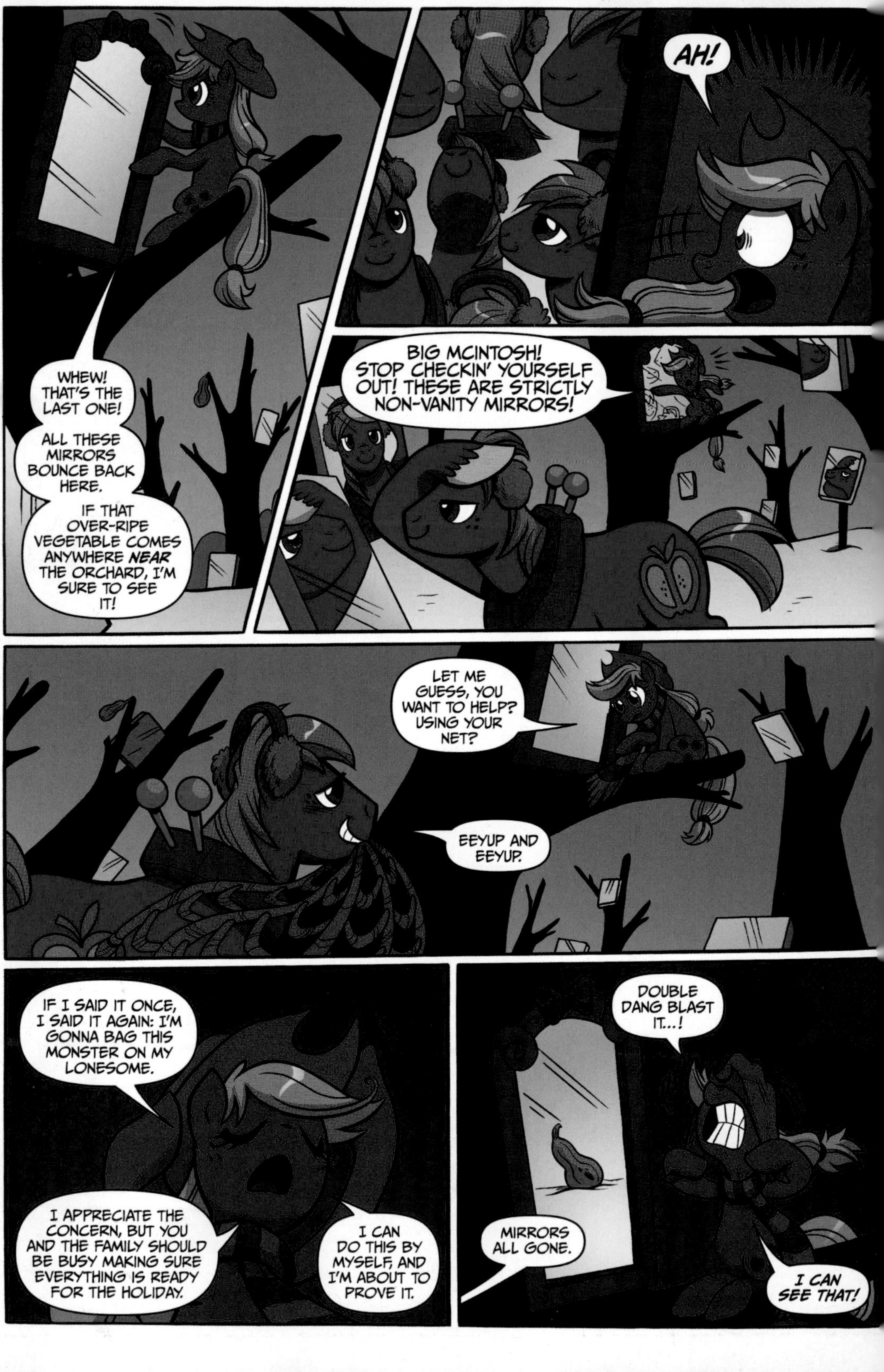
WHEW! THAT'S THE LAST ONE!
ALL THESE MIRRORS BOUNCE BACK HERE.
IF THAT OVER-RIPE VEGETABLE COMES ANYWHERE NEAR THE ORCHARD, I'M SURE TO SEE IT!
AH!
BIG MCINTOSH! STOP CHECKIN' YOURSELF OUT! THESE ARE STRICTLY NON-VANITY MIRRORS!
LET ME GUESS, YOU WANT TO HELP? USING YOUR NET?
EEYUP AND EEYUP.
IF I SAID IT ONCE, I SAID IT AGAIN: I'M GONNA BAG THIS MONSTER ON MY LONESOME.
I APPRECIATE THE CONCERN, BUT YOU AND THE FAMILY SHOULD BE BUSY MAKING SURE EVERYTHING IS READY FOR THE HOLIDAY.
I CAN DO THIS BY MYSELF, AND I'M ABOUT TO PROVE IT.
DOUBLE DANG BLAST IT...!
MIRRORS ALL GONE.
I CAN SEE THAT!

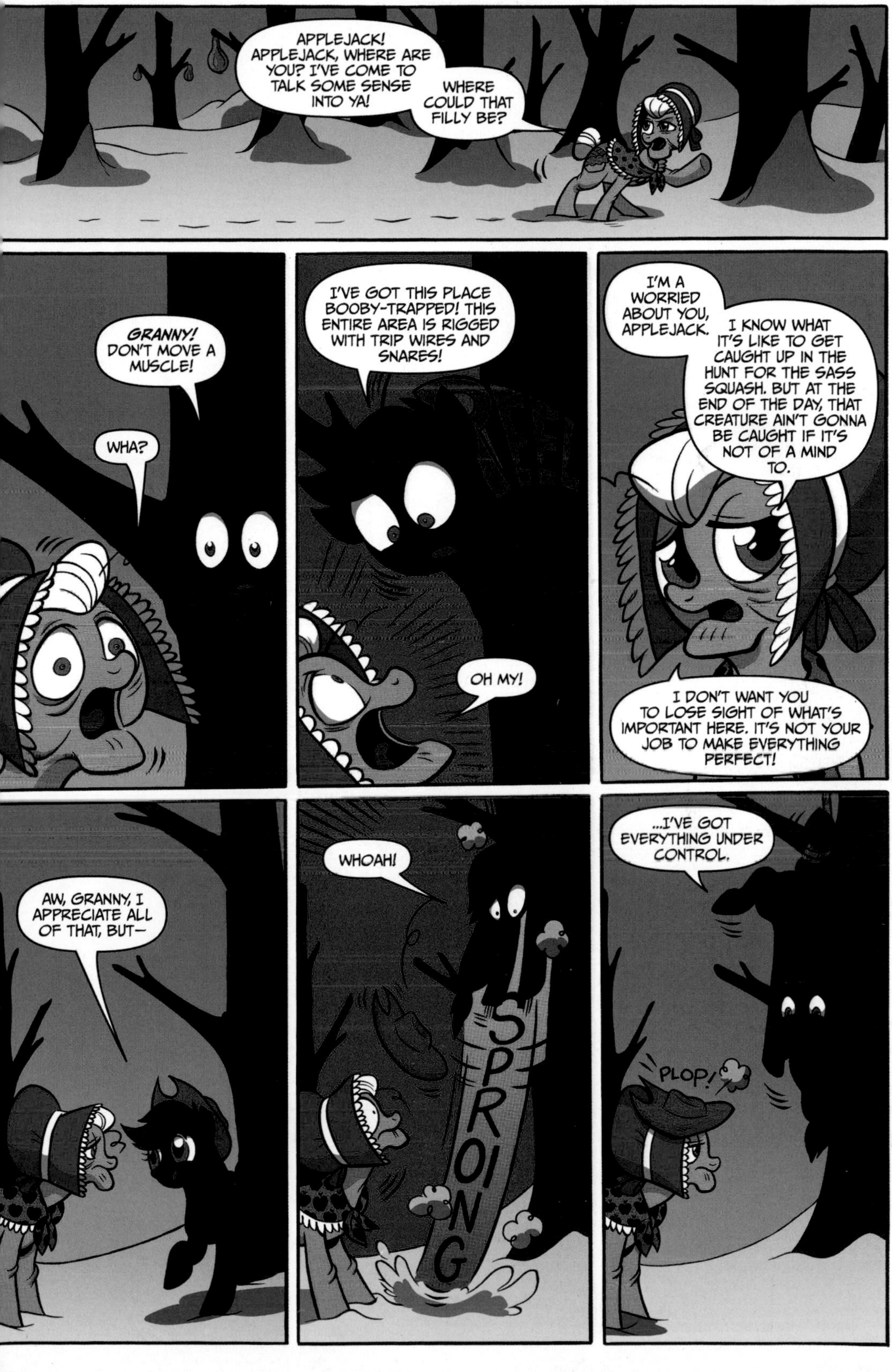

APPLEJACK! APPLEJACK, WHERE ARE YOU? I'VE COME TO TALK SOME SENSE INTO YA!
WHERE COULD THAT FILLY BE?
GRANNY! DON'T MOVE A MUSCLE!
WHA?
I'VE GOT THIS PLACE BOOBY-TRAPPED! THIS ENTIRE AREA IS RIGGED WITH TRIP WIRES AND SNARES!
OH MY!
I'M A WORRIED ABOUT YOU, APPLEJACK.
I KNOW WHAT IT'S LIKE TO GET CAUGHT UP IN THE HUNT FOR THE SASS SQUASH. BUT AT THE END OF THE DAY, THAT CREATURE AIN'T GONNA BE CAUGHT IF IT'S NOT OF A MIND TO.
I DON'T WANT YOU TO LOSE SIGHT OF WHAT'S IMPORTANT HERE. IT'S NOT YOUR JOB TO MAKE EVERYTHING PERFECT!
AW, GRANNY, I APPRECIATE ALL OF THAT, BUT—
WHOAH!
SPROING
...I'VE GOT EVERYTHING UNDER CONTROL.
PLOP!

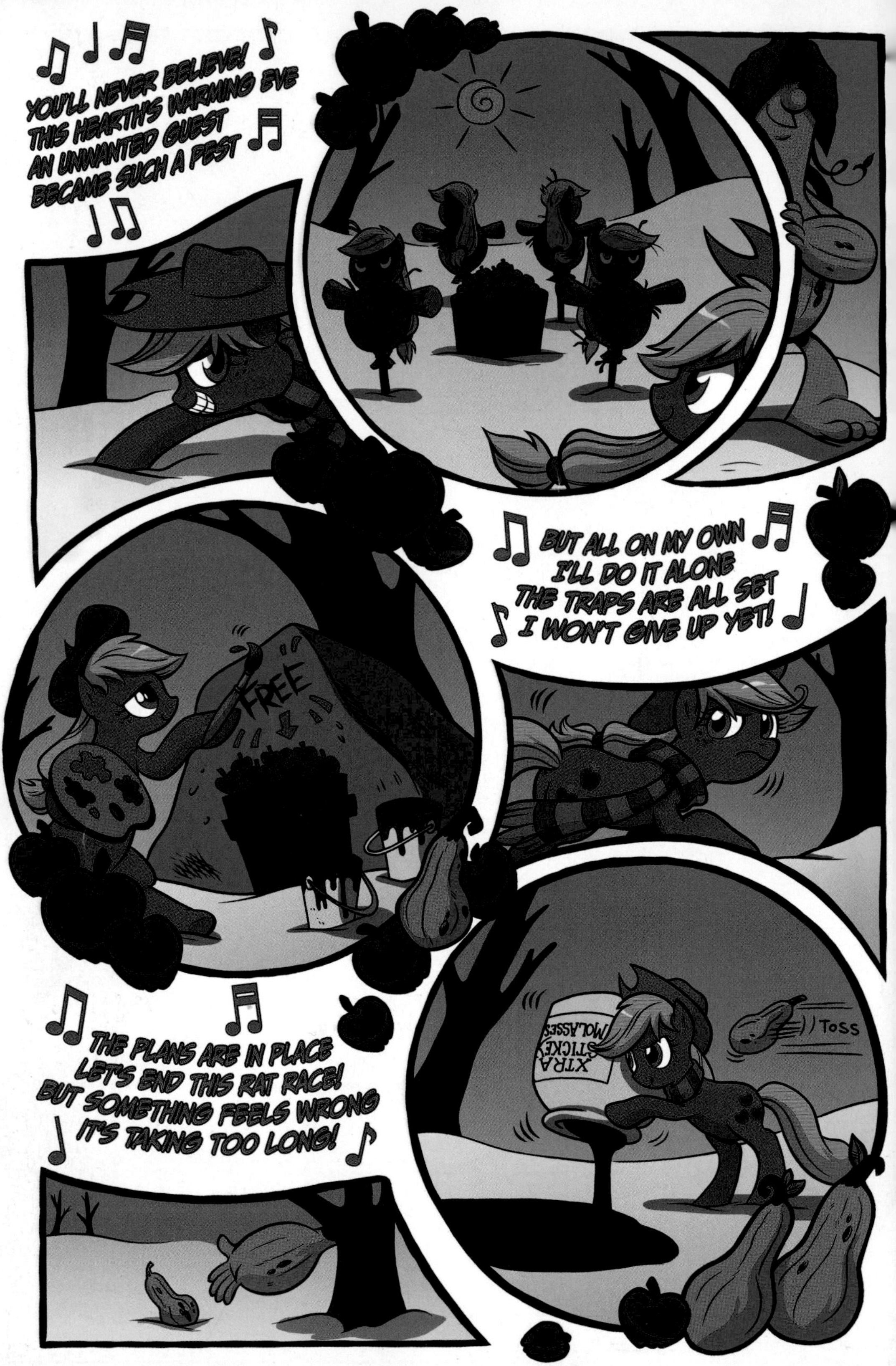
YOU'LL NEVER BELIEVE! THIS HEARTH'S WARMING EVE AN UNWANTED GUEST BECAME SUCH A PEST
BUT ALL ON MY OWN I'LL DO IT ALONE THE TRAPS ARE ALL SET I WON'T GIVE UP YET!
FREE
THE PLANS ARE IN PLACE LET'S END THIS RAT RACE! BUT SOMETHING FEELS WRONG IT'S TAKING TOO LONG!
XTRA STICKY MOLASSES
TOSS

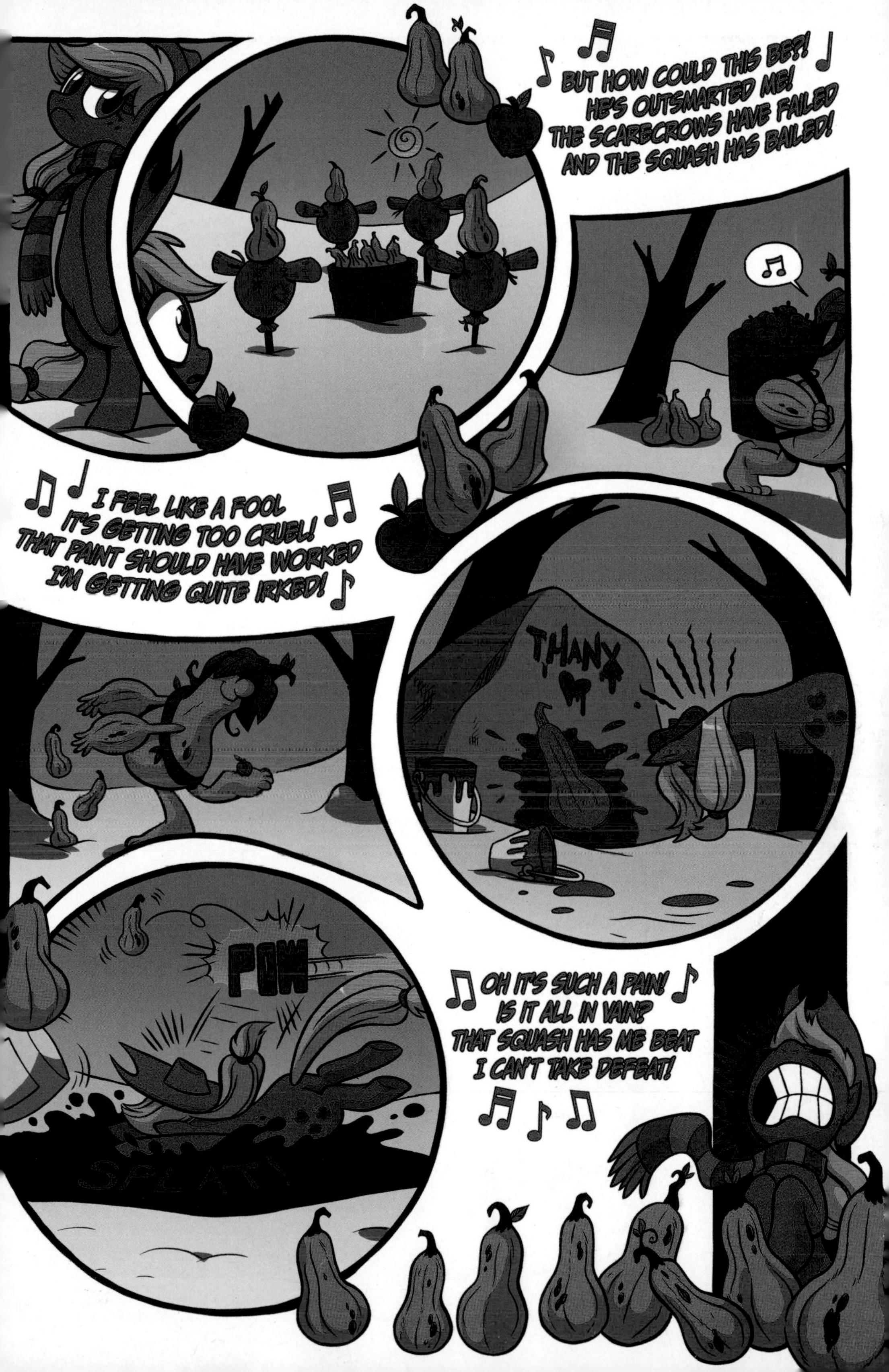
BUT HOW COULD THIS BE?! HE'S OUTSMARTED ME! THE SCARECROWS HAVE FAILED AND THE SQUASH HAS BAILED!
I FEEL LIKE A FOOL IT'S GETTING TOO CRUEL! THAT PAINT SHOULD HAVE WORKED I'M GETTING QUITE IRKED!
THANX
POW
SPLAT
OH IT'S SUCH A PAIN! IS IT ALL IN VAIN? THAT SQUASH HAS ME BEAT I CAN'T TAKE DEFEAT!

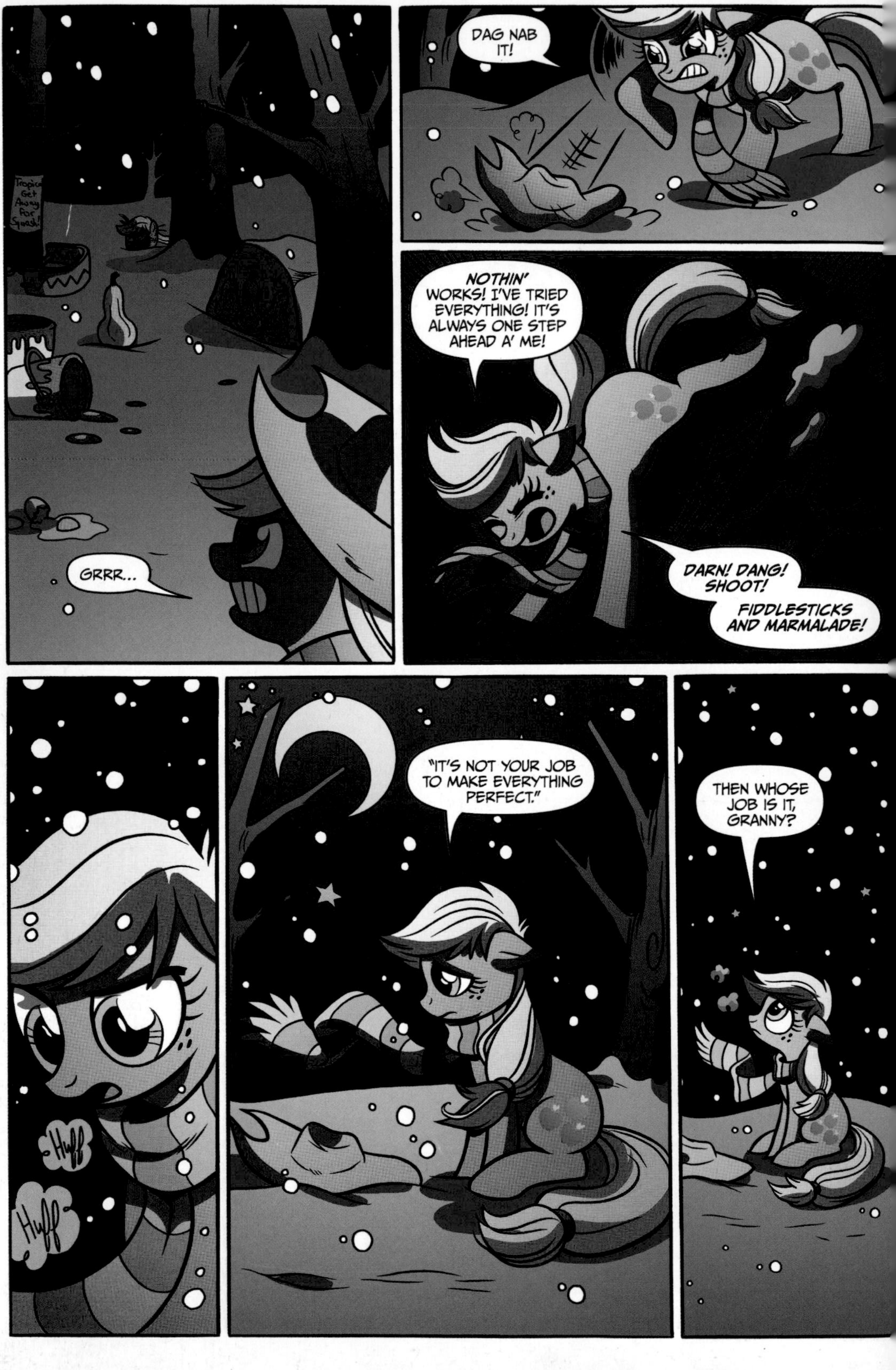
GRRR...
DAG NAB IT!
NOTHIN' WORKS! I'VE TRIED EVERYTHING! IT'S ALWAYS ONE STEP AHEAD A' ME!
DARN! DANG! SHOOT!
FIDDLESTICKS AND MARMALADE!
Huff
Huff
"IT'S NOT YOUR JOB TO MAKE EVERYTHING PERFECT."
THEN WHOSE JOB IS IT, GRANNY?

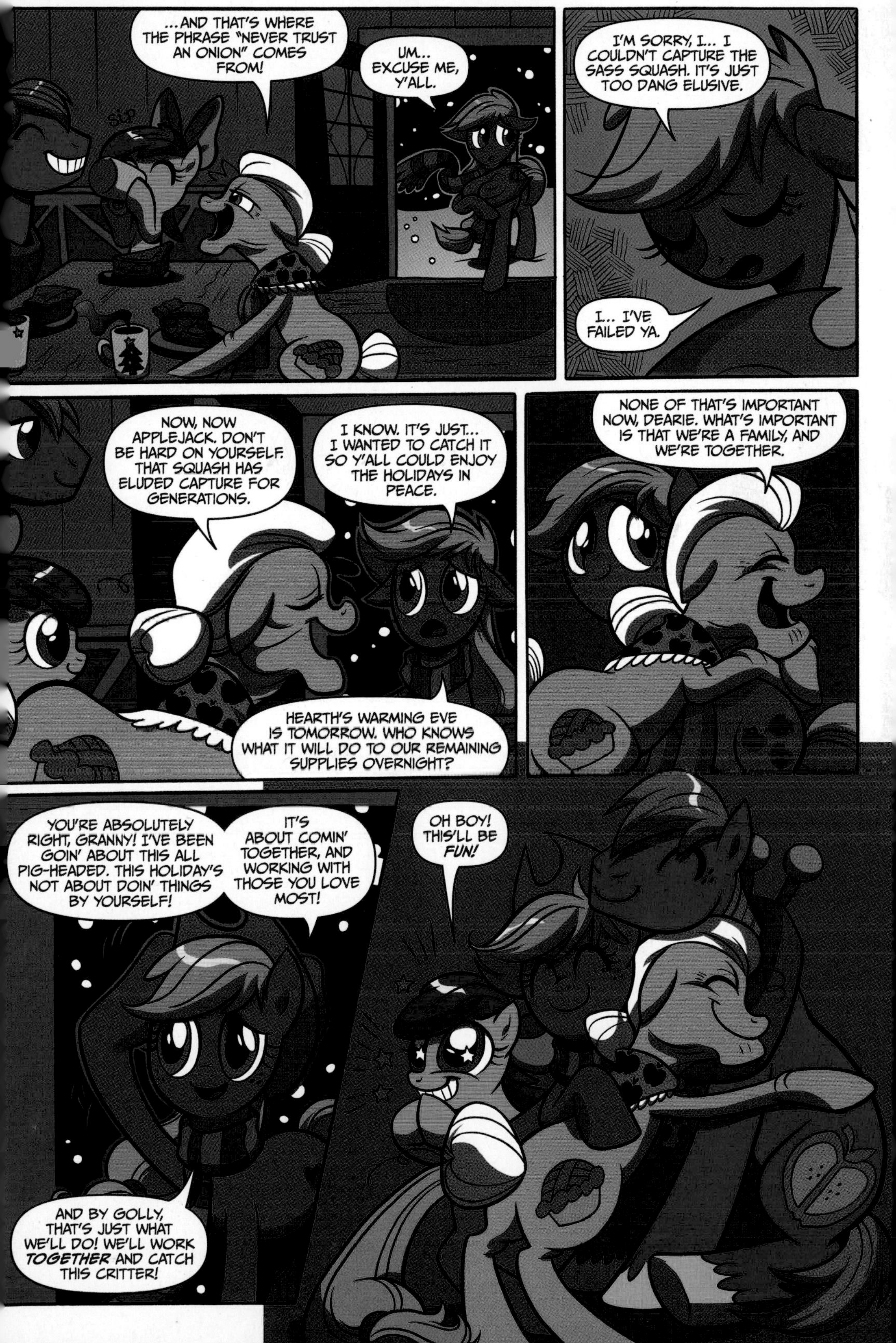
...AND THAT'S WHERE THE PHRASE "NEVER TRUST AN ONION" COMES FROM!
SIP
UM... EXCUSE ME, Y'ALL.
I'M SORRY, I... I COULDN'T CAPTURE THE SASS SQUASH. IT'S JUST TOO DANG ELUSIVE.
I... I'VE FAILED YA.
NOW, NOW APPLEJACK. DON'T BE HARD ON YOURSELF. THAT SQUASH HAS ELUDED CAPTURE FOR GENERATIONS.
I KNOW. IT'S JUST... I WANTED TO CATCH IT SO Y'ALL COULD ENJOY THE HOLIDAYS IN PEACE.
HEARTH'S WARMING EVE IS TOMORROW. WHO KNOWS WHAT IT WILL DO TO OUR REMAINING SUPPLIES OVERNIGHT?
NONE OF THAT'S IMPORTANT NOW, DEARIE. WHAT'S IMPORTANT IS THAT WE'RE A FAMILY, AND WE'RE TOGETHER.
YOU'RE ABSOLUTELY RIGHT, GRANNY! I'VE BEEN GOIN' ABOUT THIS ALL PIG-HEADED. THIS HOLIDAY'S NOT ABOUT DOIN' THINGS BY YOURSELF!
IT'S ABOUT COMIN' TOGETHER, AND WORKING WITH THOSE YOU LOVE MOST!
OH BOY! THIS'LL BE FUN!
AND BY GOLLY, THAT'S JUST WHAT WE'LL DO! WE'LL WORK TOGETHER AND CATCH THIS CRITTER!

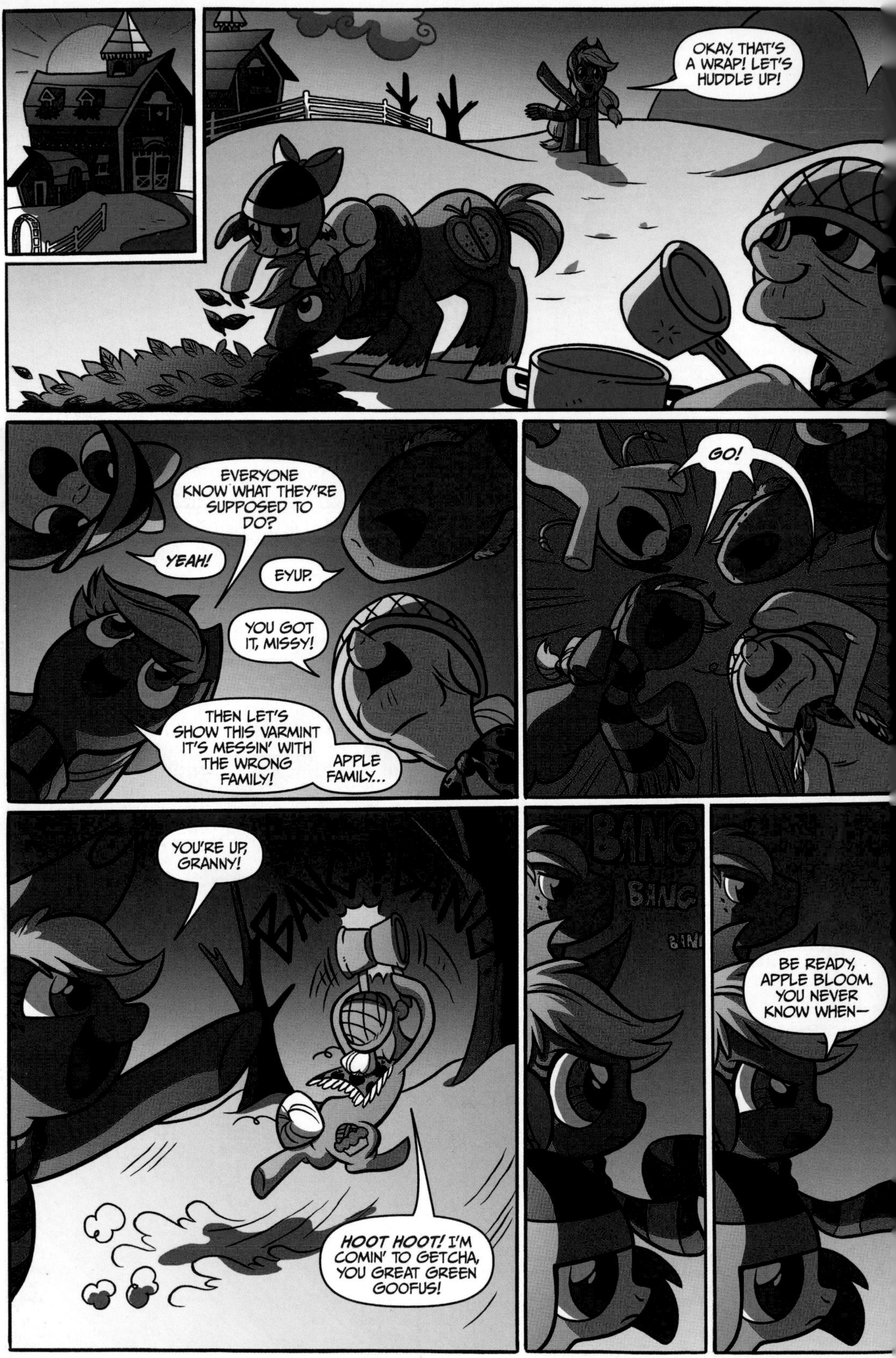
OKAY, THAT'S A WRAP! LET'S HUDDLE UP!
EVERYONE KNOW WHAT THEY'RE SUPPOSED TO DO?
YEAH!
EYUP.
YOU GOT IT, MISSY!
THEN LET'S SHOW THIS VARMINT IT'S MESSIN' WITH THE WRONG FAMILY!
APPLE FAMILY...
GO!
YOU'RE UP, GRANNY!
BANG BANG
HOOT HOOT! I'M COMIN' TO GETCHA, YOU GREAT GREEN GOOFUS!
BANG
BANG
BE READY, APPLE BLOOM. YOU NEVER KNOW WHEN—

GRAH!

GURH?

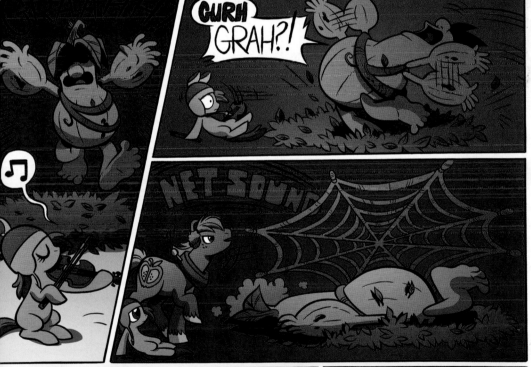

GURH GRAH?!

NET SOUND

♪

WE GOT 'EM! WE GOT 'EM! WE—

HUH? WHAT'S IT DOIN'?

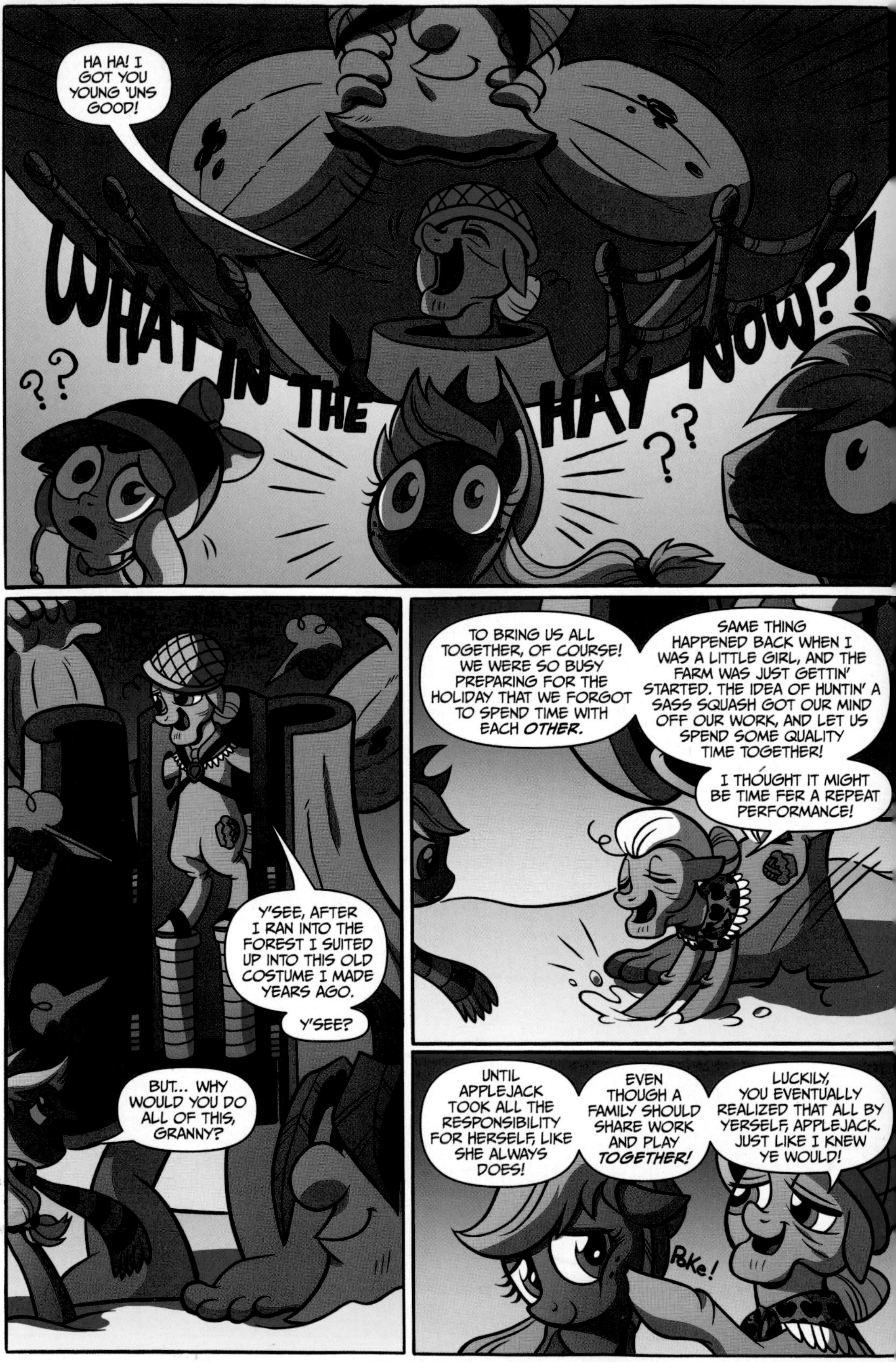
HA HA! I GOT YOU YOUNG 'UNS GOOD!
WHAT IN THE HAY NOW?!
Y'SEE, AFTER I RAN INTO THE FOREST I SUITED UP INTO THIS OLD COSTUME I MADE YEARS AGO.
Y'SEE?
BUT... WHY WOULD YOU DO ALL OF THIS, GRANNY?
TO BRING US ALL TOGETHER, OF COURSE! WE WERE SO BUSY PREPARING FOR THE HOLIDAY THAT WE FORGOT TO SPEND TIME WITH EACH *OTHER.*
SAME THING HAPPENED BACK WHEN I WAS A LITTLE GIRL, AND THE FARM WAS JUST GETTIN' STARTED. THE IDEA OF HUNTIN' A SASS SQUASH GOT OUR MIND OFF OUR WORK, AND LET US SPEND SOME QUALITY TIME TOGETHER!
I THOUGHT IT MIGHT BE TIME FER A REPEAT PERFORMANCE!
UNTIL APPLEJACK TOOK ALL THE RESPONSIBILITY FOR HERSELF, LIKE SHE ALWAYS DOES!
EVEN THOUGH A FAMILY SHOULD SHARE WORK AND PLAY *TOGETHER!*
LUCKILY, YOU EVENTUALLY REALIZED THAT ALL BY YERSELF, APPLEJACK. JUST LIKE I KNEW YE WOULD!
POKE!

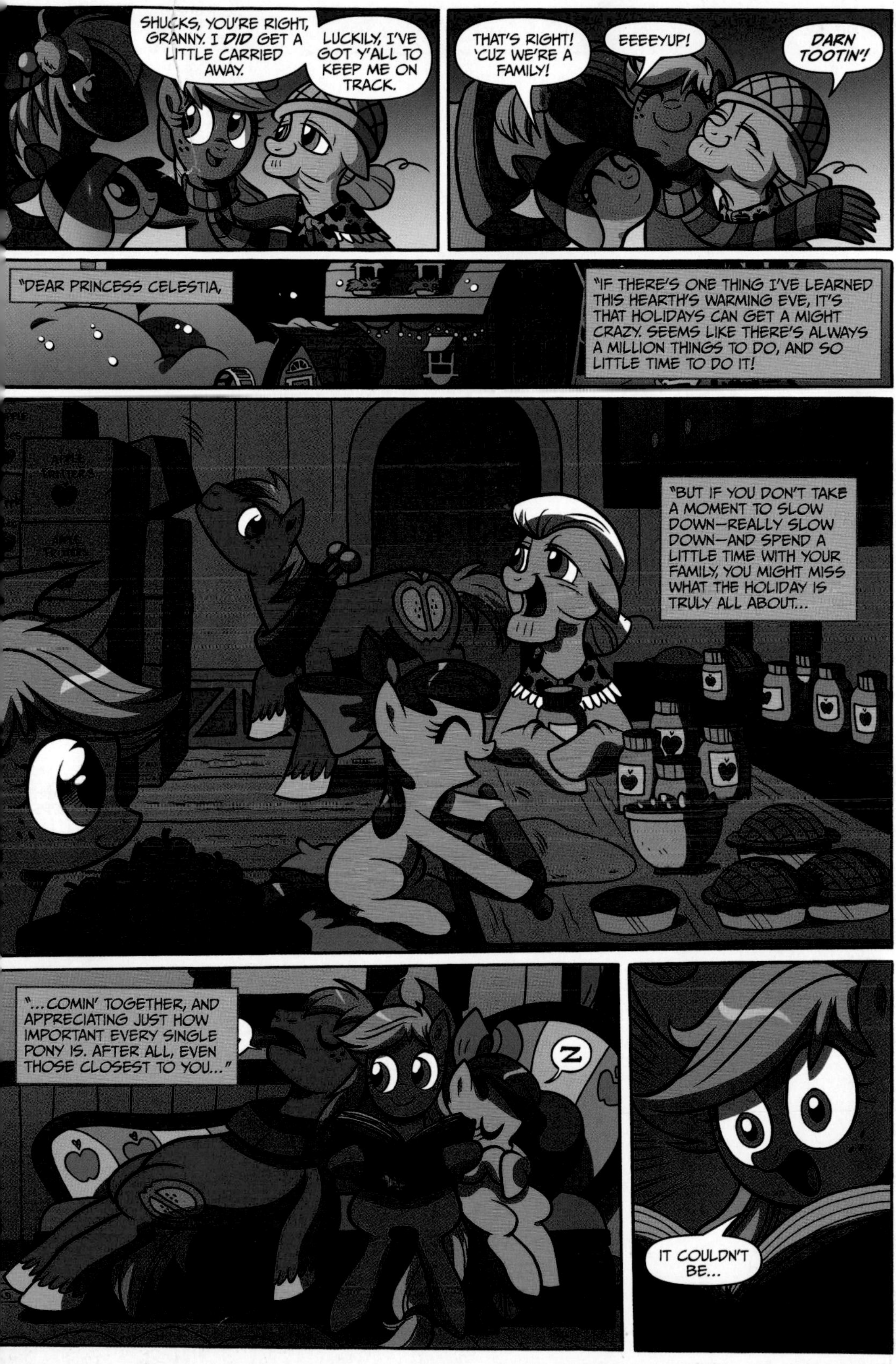
SHUCKS, YOU'RE RIGHT, GRANNY. I *DID* GET A LITTLE CARRIED AWAY.
LUCKILY, I'VE GOT Y'ALL TO KEEP ME ON TRACK.
THAT'S RIGHT! 'CUZ WE'RE A FAMILY!
EEEEYUP!
DARN TOOTIN'!
"DEAR PRINCESS CELESTIA,
"IF THERE'S ONE THING I'VE LEARNED THIS HEARTH'S WARMING EVE, IT'S THAT HOLIDAYS CAN GET A MIGHT CRAZY. SEEMS LIKE THERE'S ALWAYS A MILLION THINGS TO DO, AND SO LITTLE TIME TO DO IT!
"BUT IF YOU DON'T TAKE A MOMENT TO SLOW DOWN—REALLY SLOW DOWN—AND SPEND A LITTLE TIME WITH YOUR FAMILY, YOU MIGHT MISS WHAT THE HOLIDAY IS TRULY ALL ABOUT...
"...COMIN' TOGETHER, AND APPRECIATING JUST HOW IMPORTANT EVERY SINGLE PONY IS. AFTER ALL, EVEN THOSE CLOSEST TO YOU..."
Z
IT COULDN'T BE...

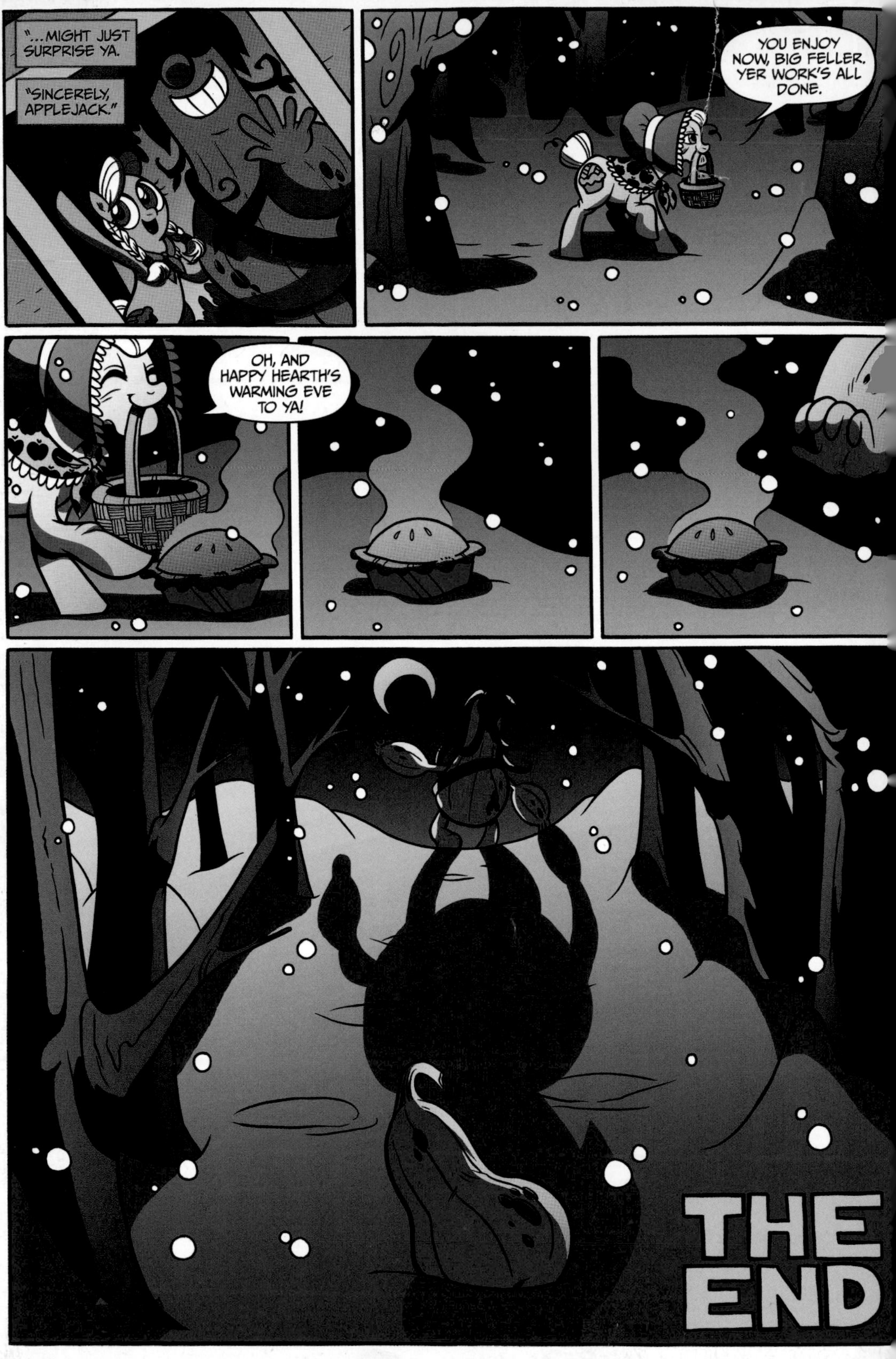
"...MIGHT JUST SURPRISE YA.
"SINCERELY, APPLEJACK."
YOU ENJOY NOW, BIG FELLER. YER WORK'S ALL DONE.
OH, AND HAPPY HEARTH'S WARMING EVE TO YA!
THE END

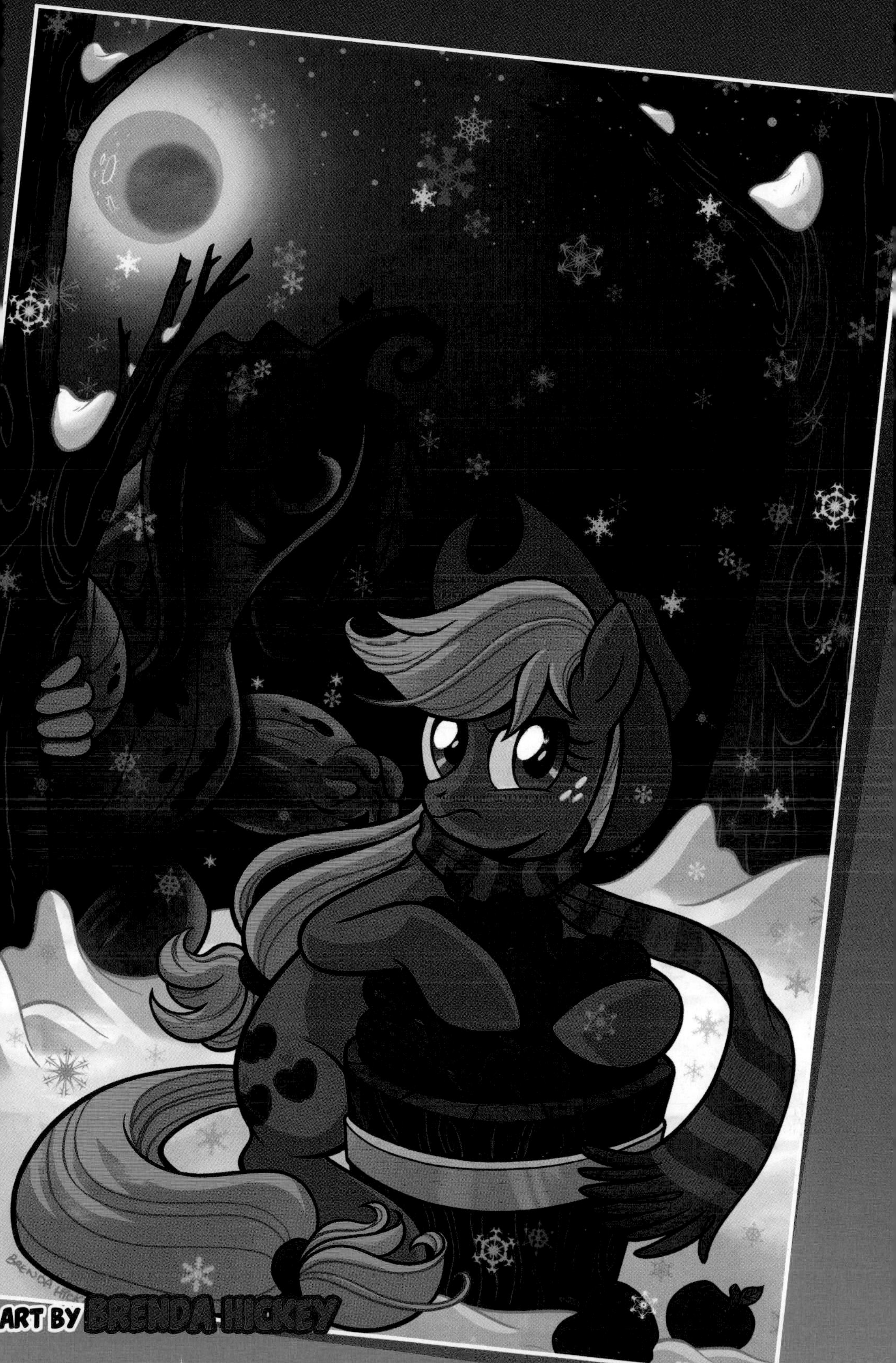
BRENDA HICKEY

ART BY BRENDA HICKEY

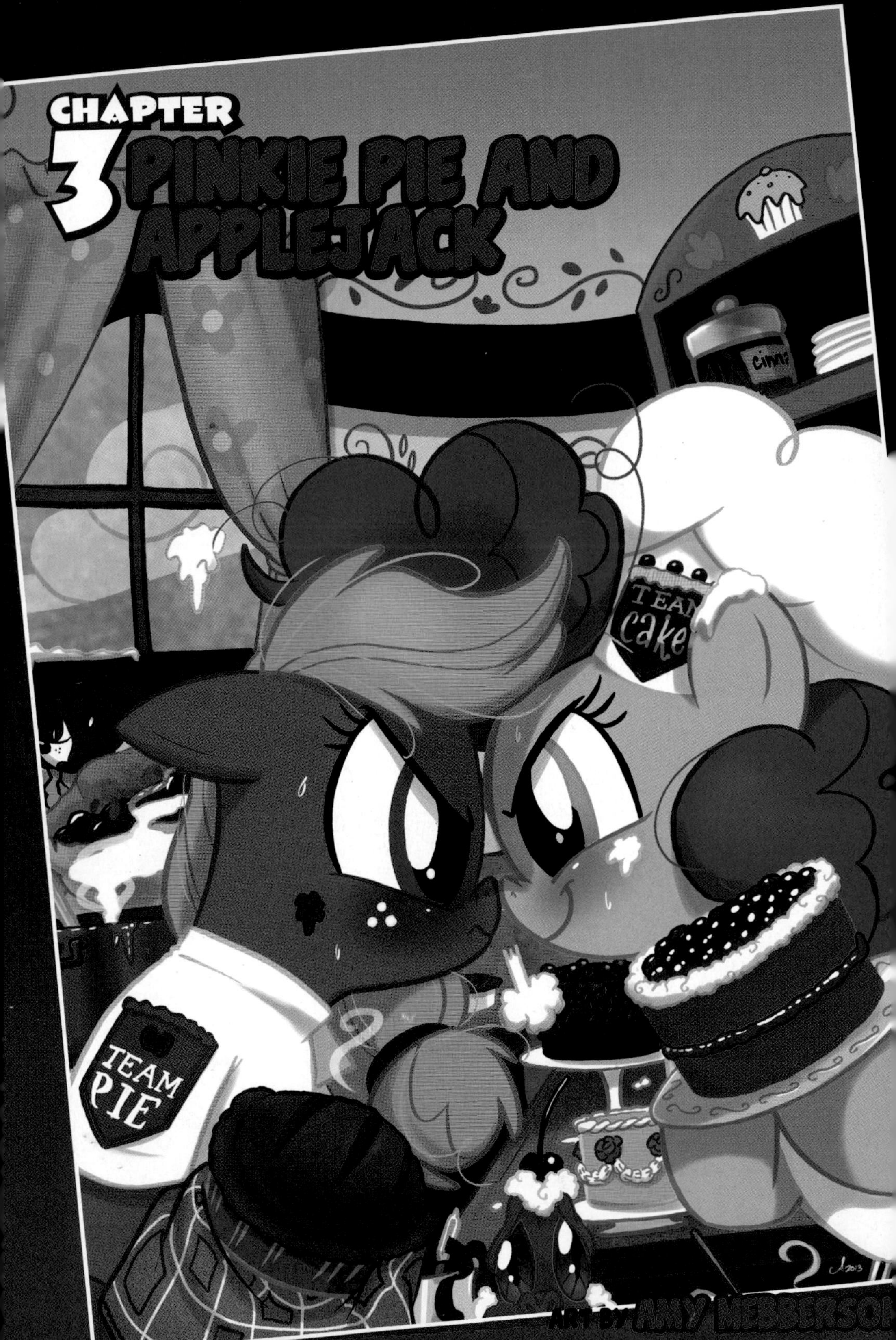
CHAPTER
3 PINKIE PIE AND APPLEJACK
cinna
TEAM cake
TEAM PIE
ART BY AMY MEBBERSO

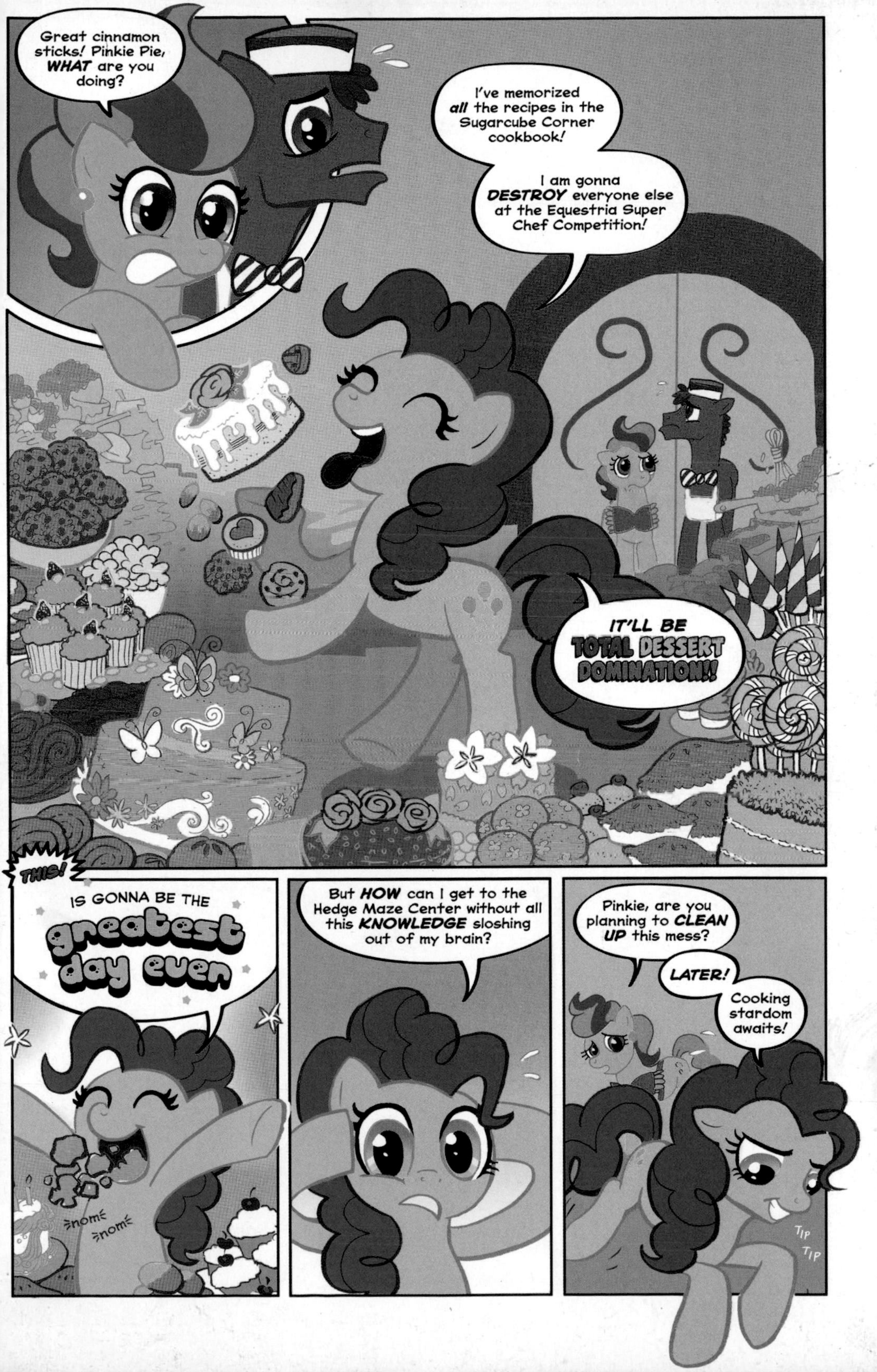

Great cinnamon sticks! Pinkie Pie, WHAT are you doing?
I've memorized all the recipes in the Sugarcube Corner cookbook!
I am gonna DESTROY everyone else at the Equestria Super Chef Competition!
IT'LL BE TOTAL DESSERT DOMINATION!!
THIS!
IS GONNA BE THE greatest day ever
nom nom
But HOW can I get to the Hedge Maze Center without all this KNOWLEDGE sloshing out of my brain?
Pinkie, are you planning to CLEAN UP this mess?
LATER!
Cooking stardom awaits!
TIP TIP

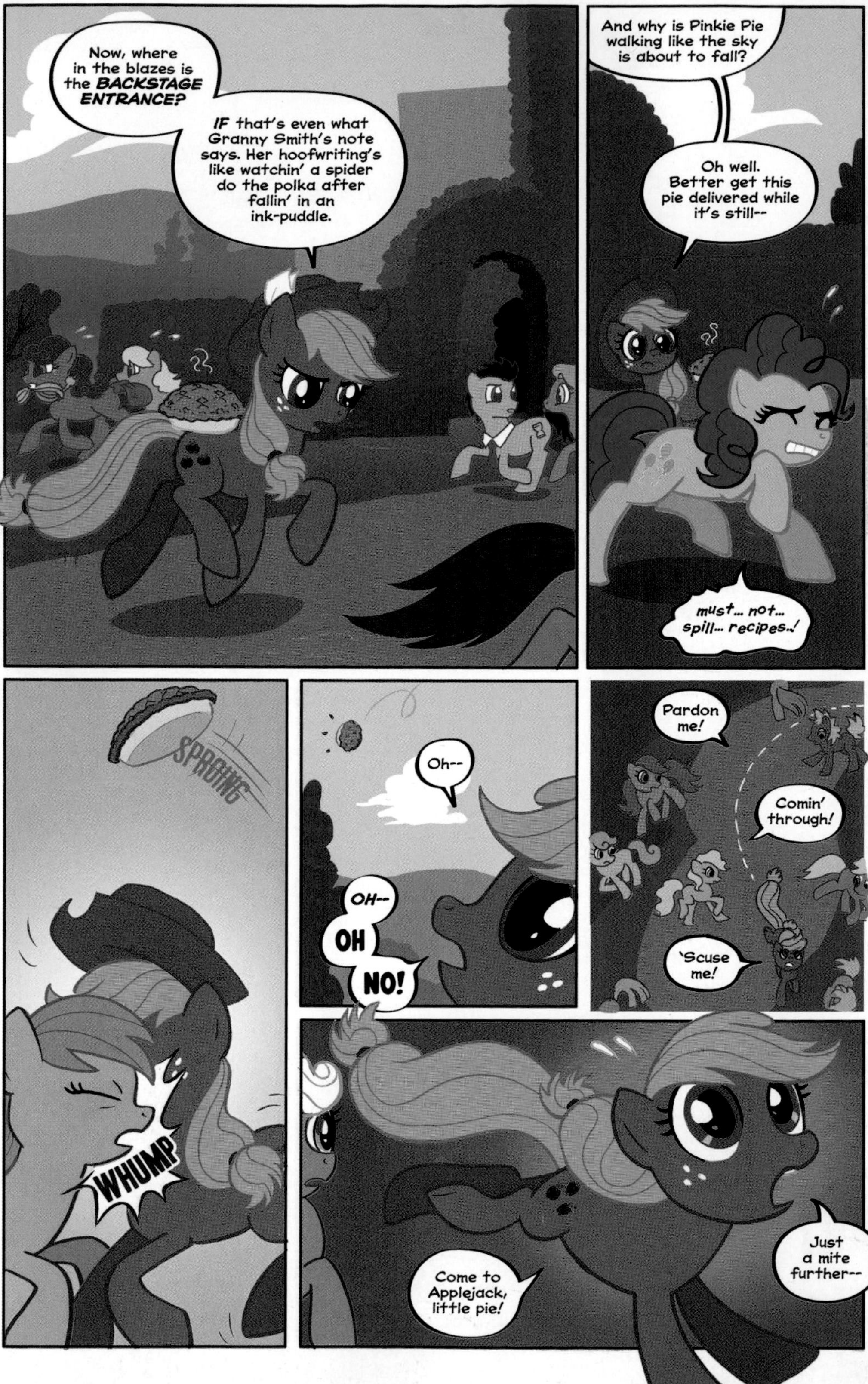
Now, where in the blazes is the BACKSTAGE ENTRANCE?
IF that's even what Granny Smith's note says. Her hoofwriting's like watchin' a spider do the polka after fallin' in an ink-puddle.
And why is Pinkie Pie walking like the sky is about to fall?
Oh well. Better get this pie delivered while it's still--
must... not... spill... recipes..!
SPROING
WHUMP
Oh--
OH--
OH
NO!
Pardon me!
Comin' through!
'Scuse me!
Come to Applejack, little pie!
Just a mite further--

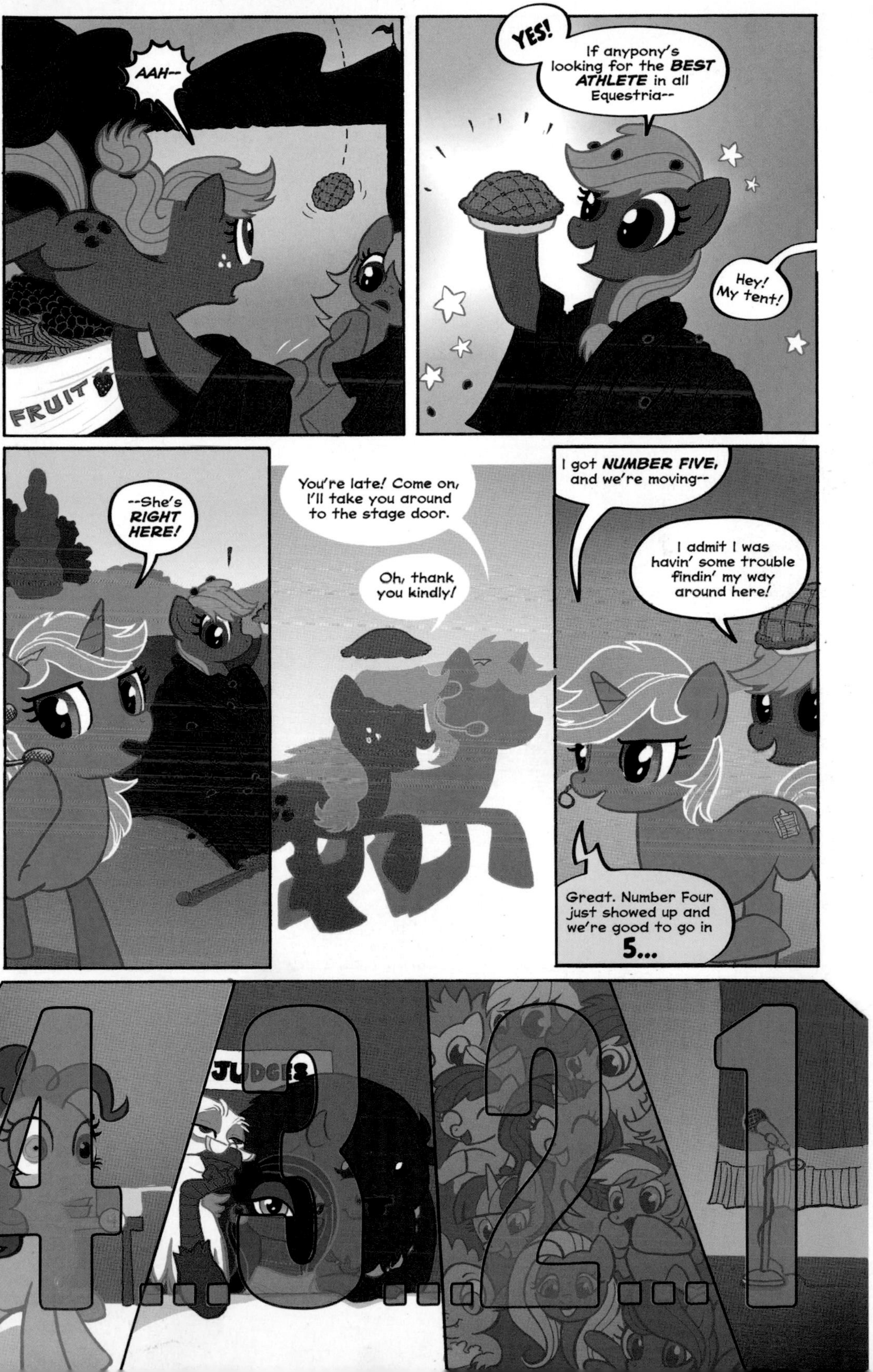

AAH--
FRUIT
YES!
If anypony's looking for the BEST ATHLETE in all Equestria--
Hey! My tent!
--She's RIGHT HERE!
You're late! Come on, I'll take you around to the stage door.
Oh, thank you kindly!
I got NUMBER FIVE, and we're moving--
I admit I was havin' some trouble findin' my way around here!
Great. Number Four just showed up and we're good to go in 5...
4...3...2...1

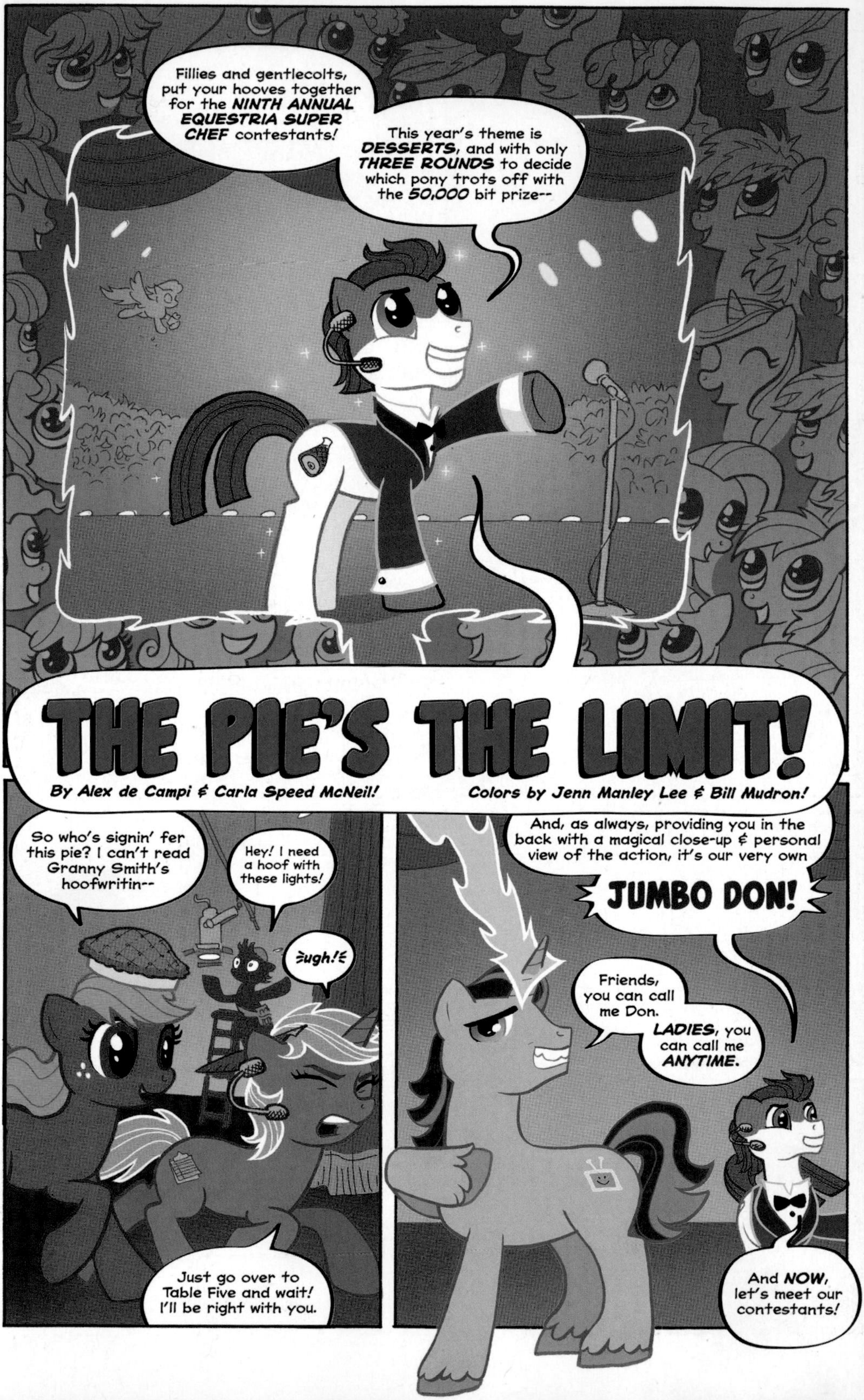
Fillies and gentlecolts, put your hooves together for the NINTH ANNUAL EQUESTRIA SUPER CHEF contestants!
This year's theme is DESSERTS, and with only THREE ROUNDS to decide which pony trots off with the 50,000 bit prize--
THE PIE'S THE LIMIT!
By Alex de Campi & Carla Speed McNeil!
Colors by Jenn Manley Lee & Bill Mudron!
So who's signin' fer this pie? I can't read Granny Smith's hoofwritin--
Hey! I need a hoof with these lights!
ugh!
Just go over to Table Five and wait! I'll be right with you.
And, as always, providing you in the back with a magical close-up & personal view of the action, it's our very own
JUMBO DON!
Friends, you can call me Don.
LADIES, you can call me ANYTIME.
And NOW, let's meet our contestants!

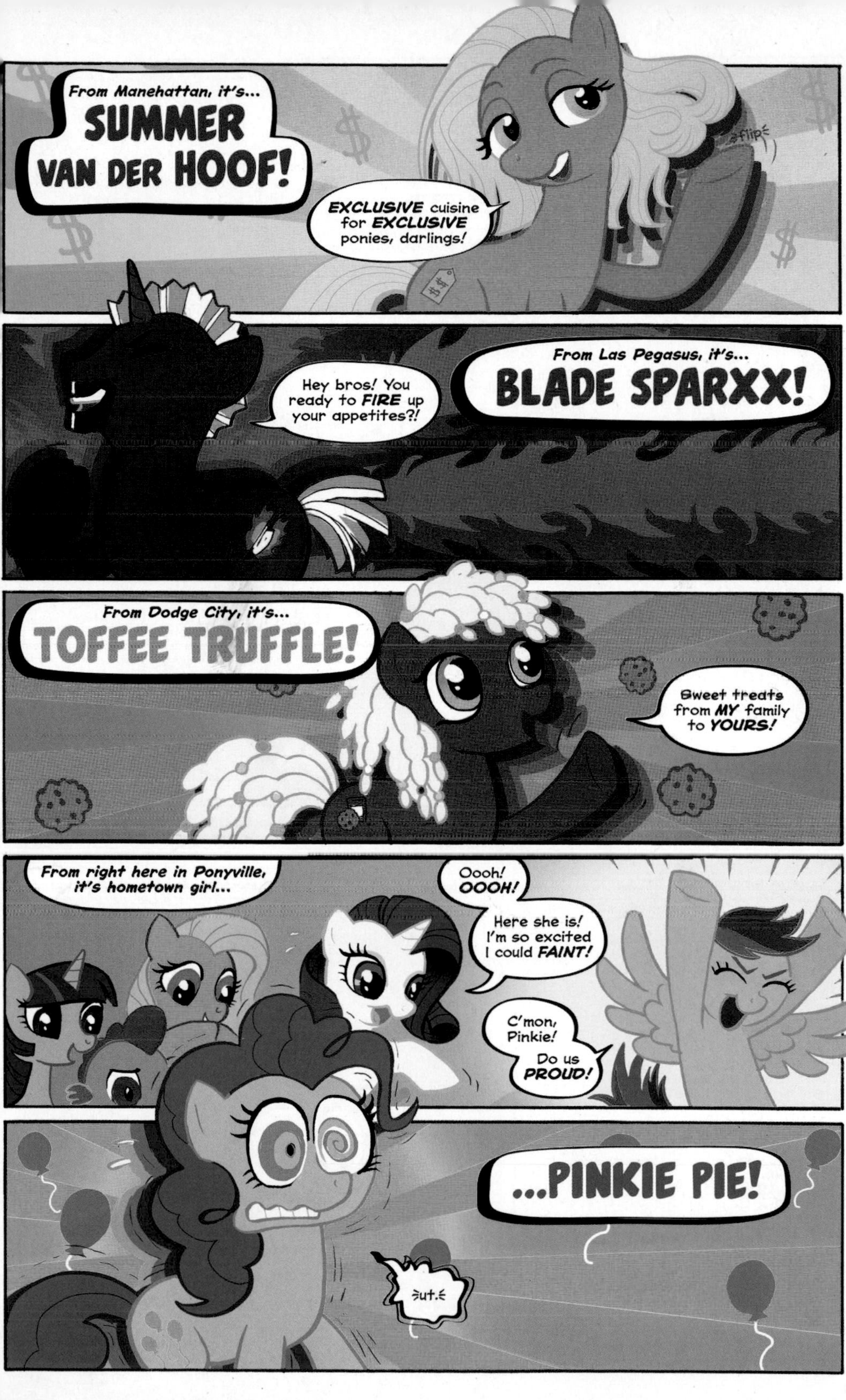
From Manehattan, it's...
SUMMER VAN DER HOOF!
flip
EXCLUSIVE cuisine for EXCLUSIVE ponies, darlings!
Hey bros! You ready to FIRE up your appetites?!
From Las Pegasus, it's...
BLADE SPARXX!
From Dodge City, it's...
TOFFEE TRUFFLE!
Sweet treats from MY family to YOURS!
From right here in Ponyville, it's hometown girl...
Oooh! OOOH!
Here she is! I'm so excited I could FAINT!
C'mon, Pinkie!
Do us PROUD!
...PINKIE PIE!
ut.

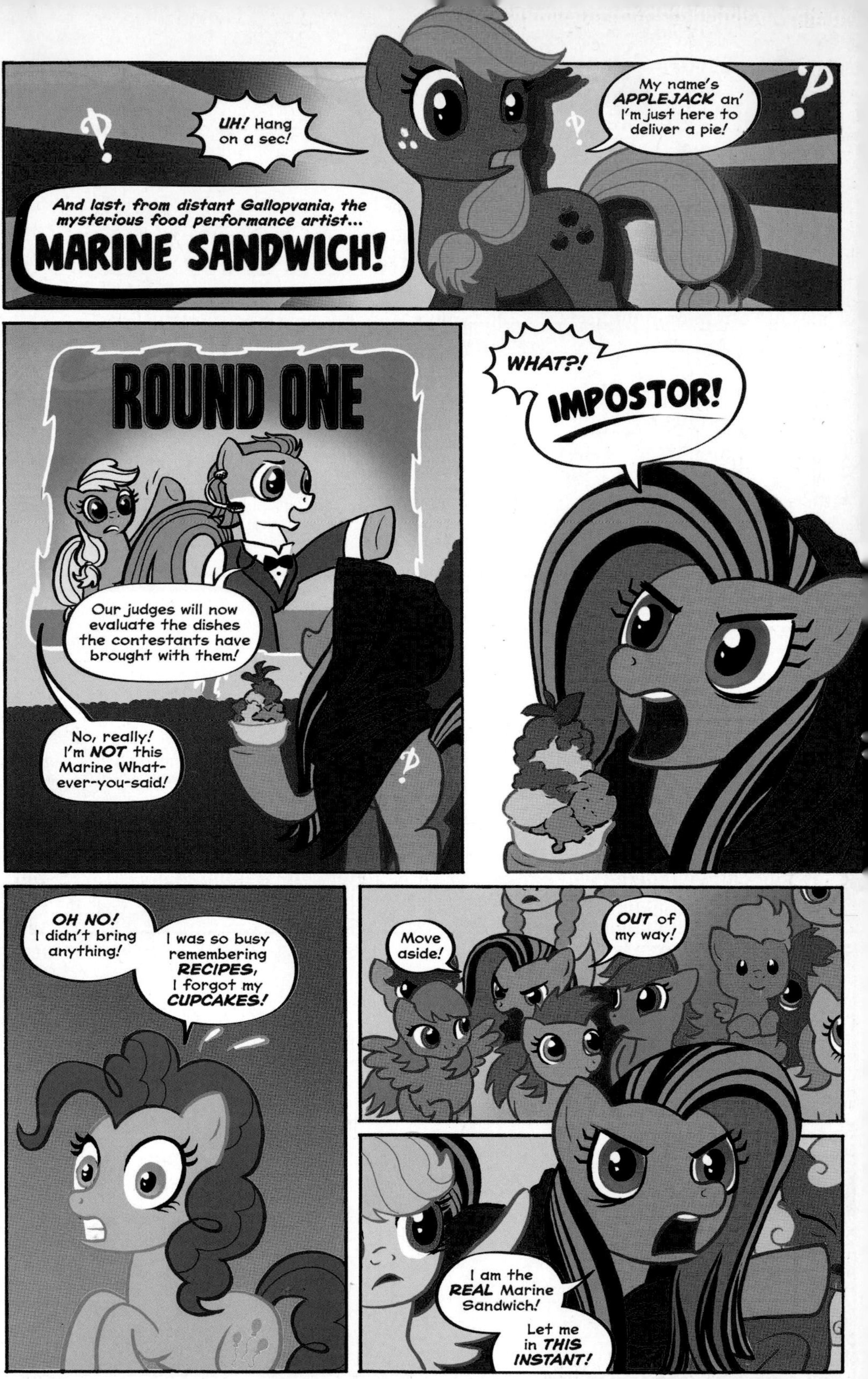
And last, from distant Gallopvania, the mysterious food performance artist...
MARINE SANDWICH!
UH! Hang on a sec!
My name's APPLEJACK an' I'm just here to deliver a pie!
ROUND ONE
Our judges will now evaluate the dishes the contestants have brought with them!
No, really! I'm NOT this Marine What-ever-you-said!
WHAT?!
IMPOSTOR!
OH NO! I didn't bring anything!
I was so busy remembering RECIPES, I forgot my CUPCAKES!
Move aside!
OUT of my way!
I am the REAL Marine Sandwich!
Let me in THIS INSTANT!

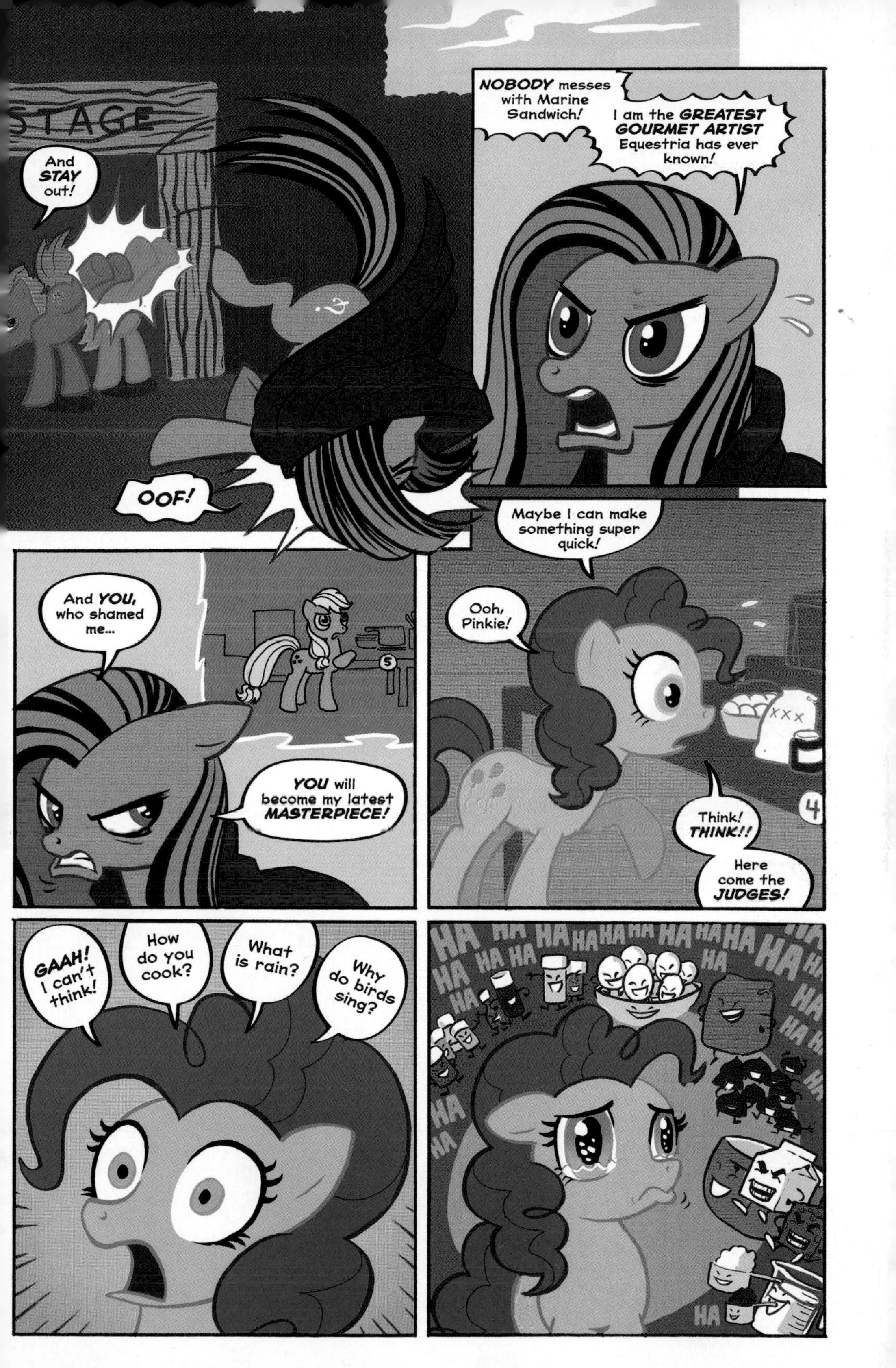
STAGE
And STAY out!
OOF!
NOBODY messes with Marine Sandwich!
I am the GREATEST GOURMET ARTIST Equestria has ever known!
And YOU, who shamed me...
YOU will become my latest MASTERPIECE!
Maybe I can make something super quick!
Ooh, Pinkie!
Think! THINK!!
Here come the JUDGES!
GAAH! I can't think!
How do you cook?
What is rain?
Why do birds sing?
HA HA HA HA HA HA HA HA HA HA HA HA HA HA HA HA HA HA HA HA HA HA HA HA

AND WITH A SURPRISINGLY SIMPLE APPLE PIE, CONCEPTUAL FOOD PRANKSTER MARINE SANDWICH WINS ROUND ONE!

I **LOVE** how you're pretending to go **COUNTRY**, Marine! **SO** unexpected!

Mmmm!

Dibs on that last piece!

≥sigh≤

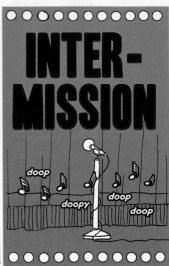

INTER-MISSION

doop

doopy

doop

doop

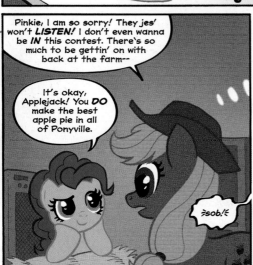

Pinkie, I am so sorry! They jes' won't **LISTEN!** I don't even wanna be **IN** this contest. There's so much to be gettin' on with back at the farm--

It's okay, Applejack! You **DO** make the best apple pie in all of Ponyville.

≥sob!≤

HUH?!

≥snif≤

OH! Hi...

You're Toffee, right?

Are you okay?

I-I'm fine.

I'm just really nervous. This is a lot more **SCARY** than I thought it would be.

You're telling me! I forgot every recipe I ever knew as soon as that spotlight hit me!

≥POOF!≤ All gone!

And I really wanted to **WIN** so I could reopen Dodge City's restaurant!

WAIT, the Cherry Pit closed down? I used to love that place when I was visitin' my kin!

YER!

Miss Bertie retired, and now families don't have anywhere to go for a treat!

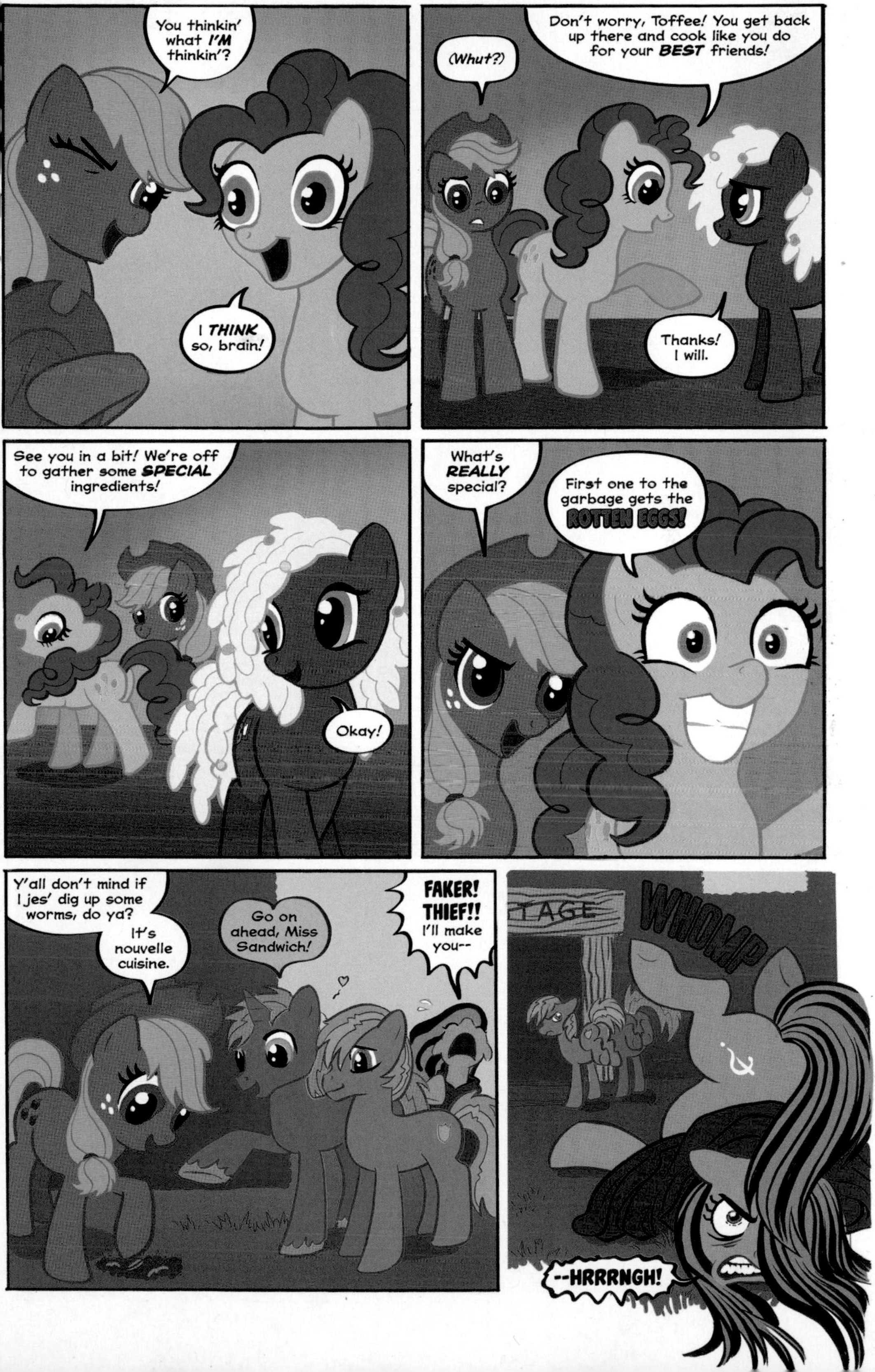
You thinkin' what I'M thinkin'?
I THINK so, brain!
(Whut?)
Don't worry, Toffee! You get back up there and cook like you do for your BEST friends!
Thanks! I will.
See you in a bit! We're off to gather some SPECIAL ingredients!
Okay!
What's REALLY special?
First one to the garbage gets the ROTTEN EGGS!
Y'all don't mind if I jes' dig up some worms, do ya?
It's nouvelle cuisine.
Go on ahead, Miss Sandwich!
FAKER! THIEF!! I'll make you--
WHOMP
--HRRRNGH!

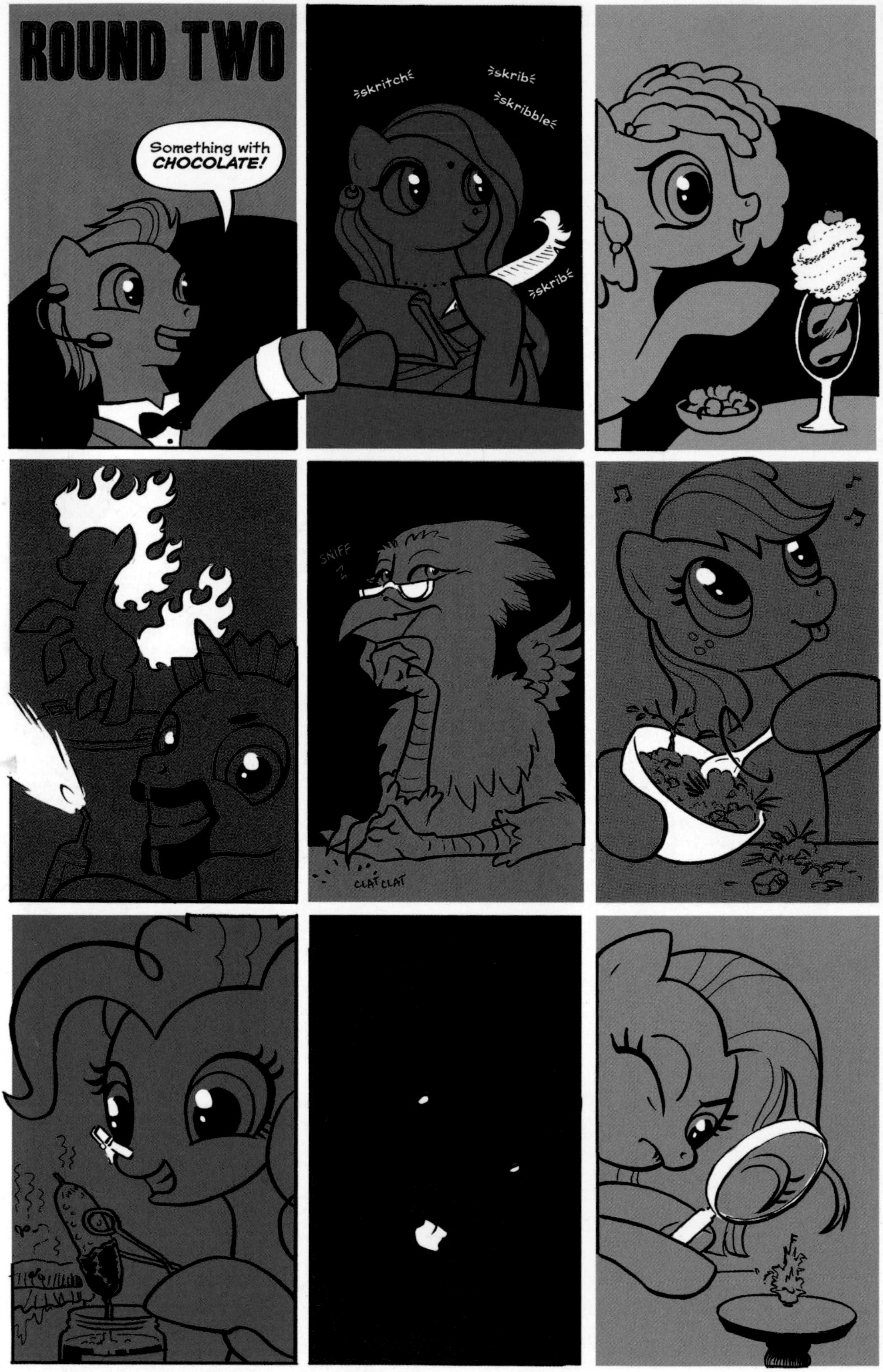
ROUND TWO
Something with CHOCOLATE!
skritch
skrib
skribble
skrib
SNIFF
CLAT CLAT

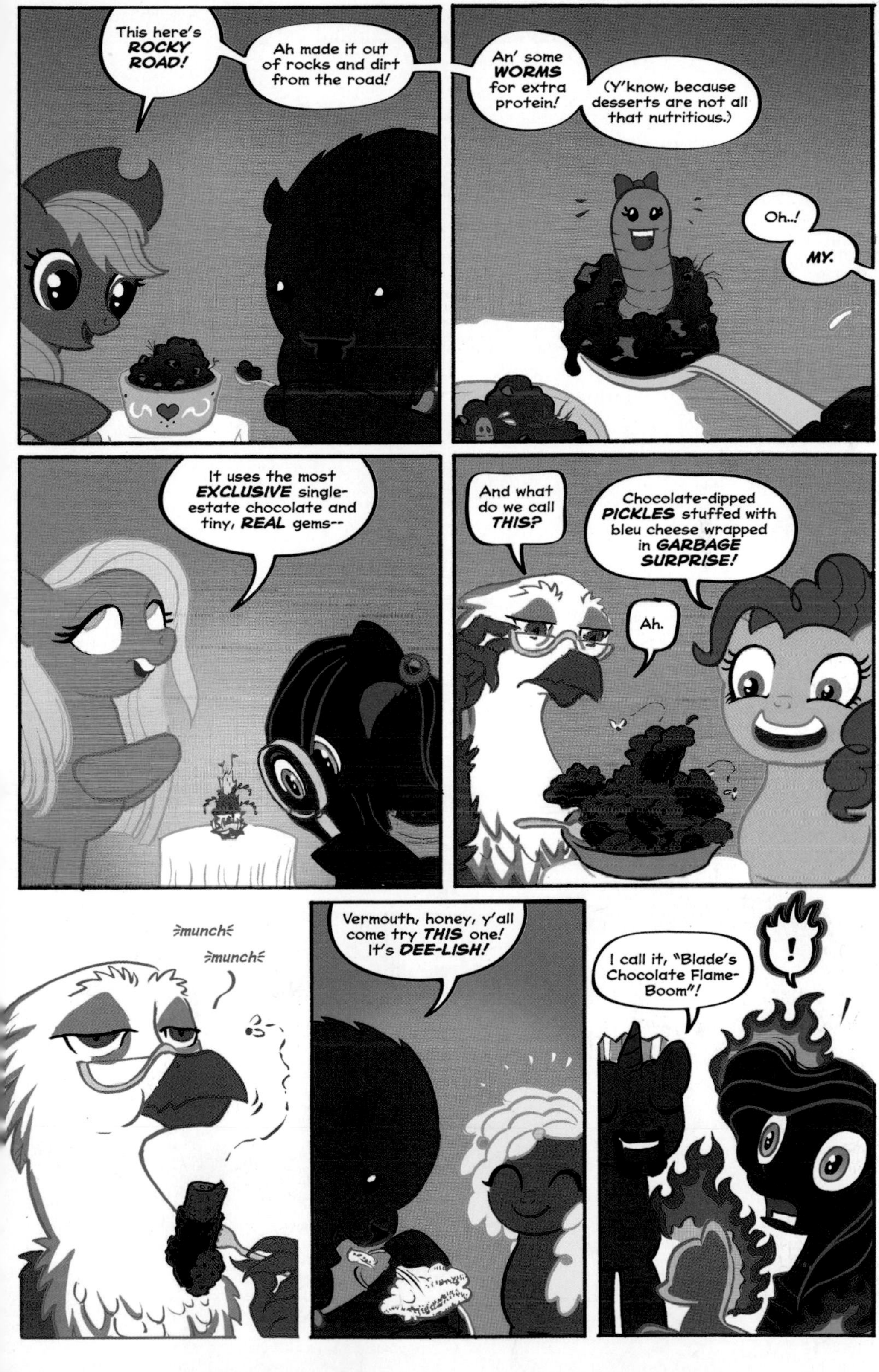
This here's ROCKY ROAD!
Ah made it out of rocks and dirt from the road!
An' some WORMS for extra protein!
(Y'know, because desserts are not all that nutritious.)
Oh..!
MY.
It uses the most EXCLUSIVE single-estate chocolate and tiny, REAL gems--
And what do we call THIS?
Chocolate-dipped PICKLES stuffed with bleu cheese wrapped in GARBAGE SURPRISE!
Ah.
munch
munch
Vermouth, honey, y'all come try THIS one! It's DEE-LISH!
I call it, "Blade's Chocolate Flame-Boom"!
!

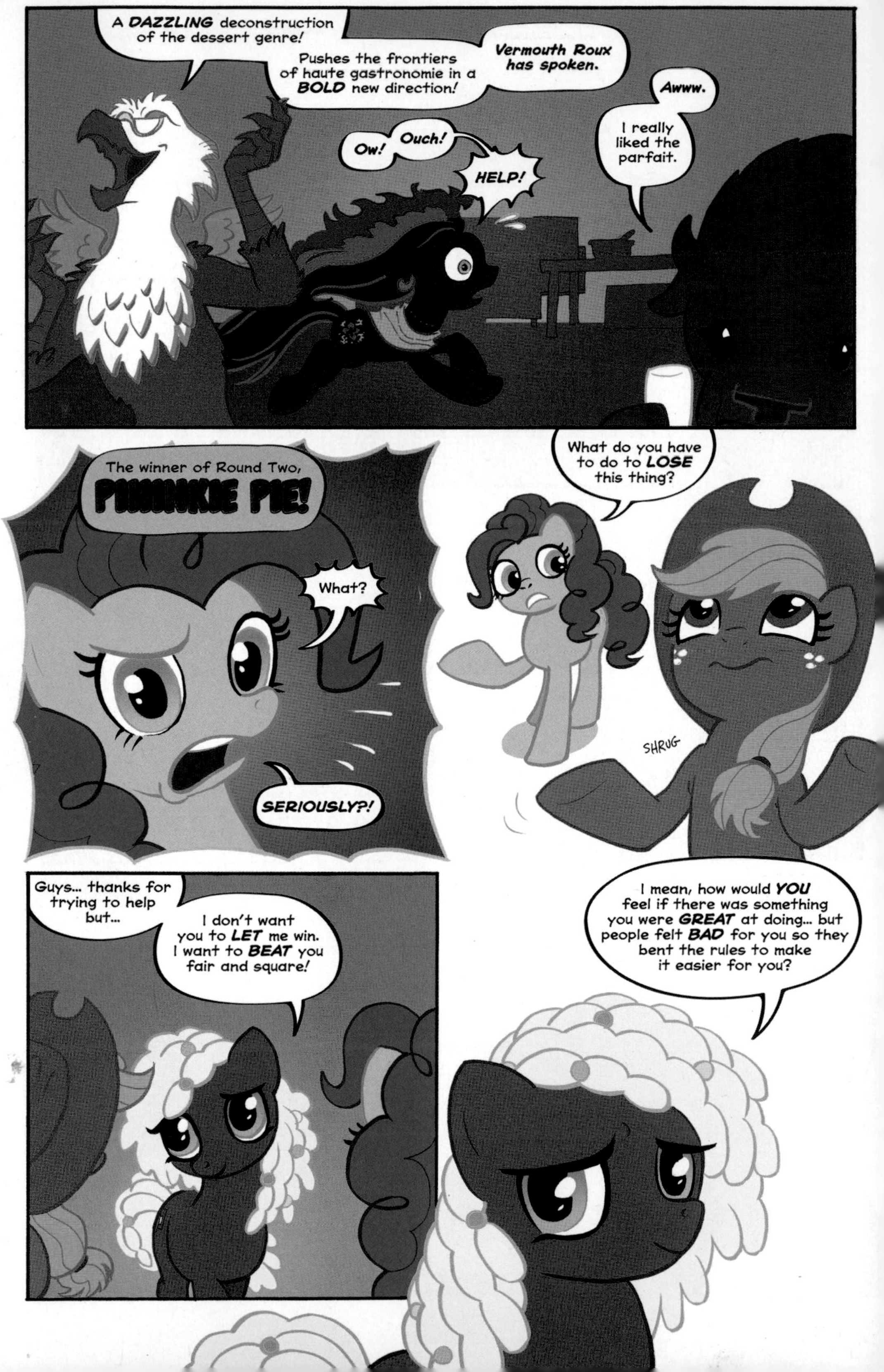
A DAZZLING deconstruction of the dessert genre!
Pushes the frontiers of haute gastronomie in a BOLD new direction!
Vermouth Roux has spoken.
Ow!
Ouch!
HELP!
Awww.
I really liked the parfait.
The winner of Round Two, PIIIINKIE PIE!
What?
SERIOUSLY?!
What do you have to do to LOSE this thing?
SHRUG
Guys... thanks for trying to help but...
I don't want you to LET me win. I want to BEAT you fair and square!
I mean, how would YOU feel if there was something you were GREAT at doing... but people felt BAD for you so they bent the rules to make it easier for you?

That would mean ponies didn't really find my jokes *FUNNY!* They'd only be laughing to make me feel better!

That would make me feel so *NOT* better!

And all my *RODEO RIBBONS* would be... not worth the ribbon they're printed on!

You're right, Toffee! May the *BEST* pony win!

As long as that pony's *ME!*

Or *ME!*

Ya know, ever since I stopped caring about winning, I'm having a *LOT* more *FUN!*

ROUND THREE

Make--

--Your *FAVORITE* recipe.

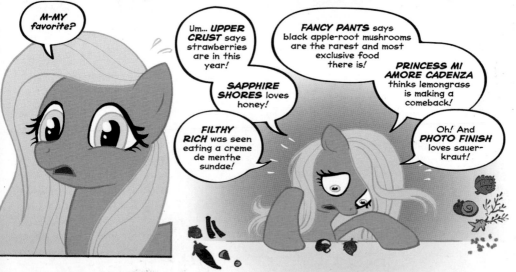

M-MY favorite?

Um... *UPPER CRUST* says strawberries are in this year!

SAPPHIRE SHORES loves honey!

FILTHY RICH was seen eating a creme de menthe sundae!

FANCY PANTS says black apple-root mushrooms are the rarest and most exclusive food there is!

PRINCESS MI AMORE CADENZA thinks lemongrass is making a comeback!

Oh! And *PHOTO FINISH* loves sauerkraut!

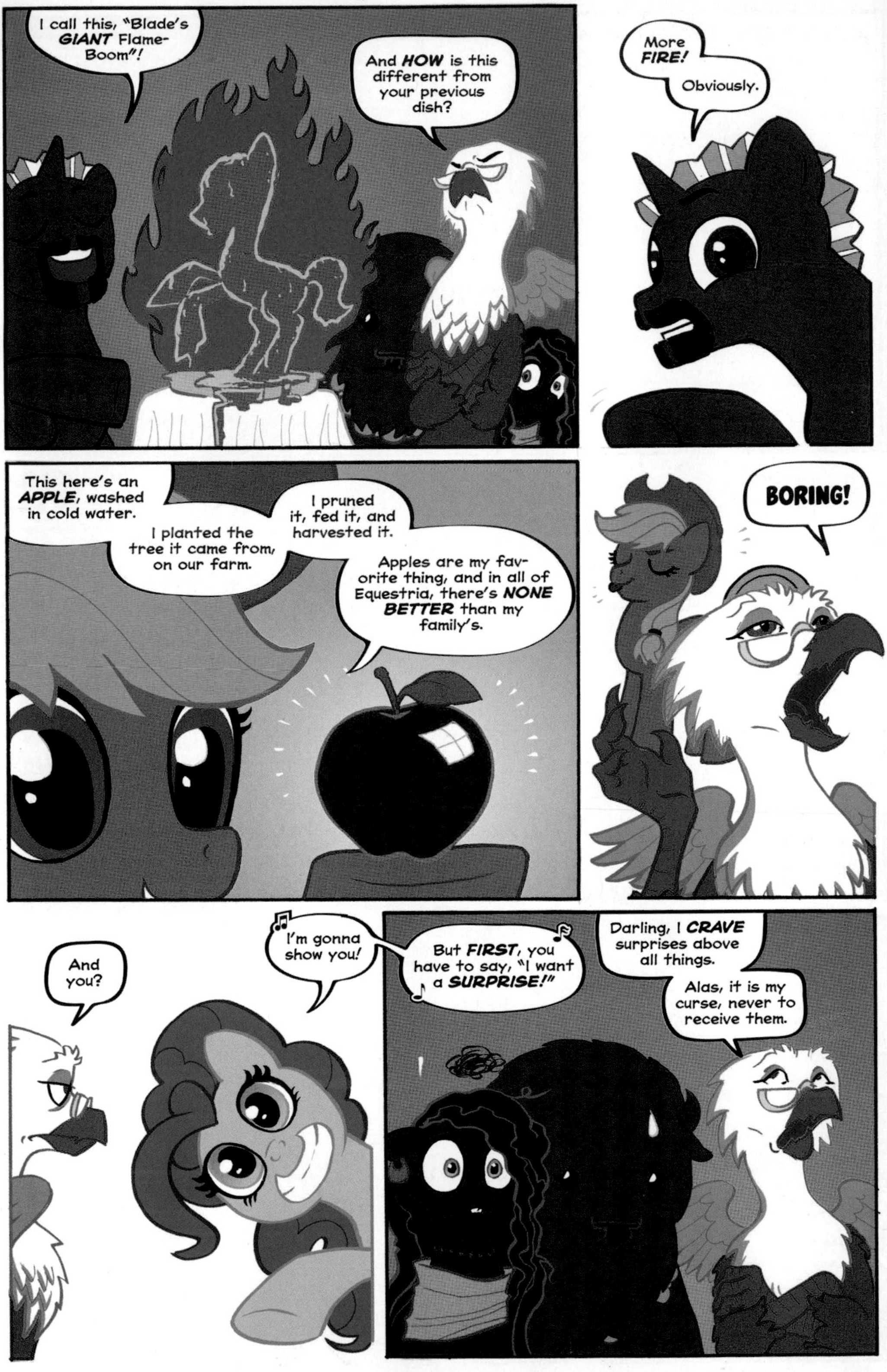
I call this, "Blade's GIANT Flame-Boom"!
And HOW is this different from your previous dish?
More FIRE!
Obviously.
This here's an APPLE, washed in cold water.
I planted the tree it came from, on our farm.
I pruned it, fed it, and harvested it.
Apples are my fav-orite thing, and in all of Equestria, there's NONE BETTER than my family's.
BORING!
And you?
I'm gonna show you!
But FIRST, you have to say, "I want a SURPRISE!"
Darling, I CRAVE surprises above all things.
Alas, it is my curse, never to receive them.

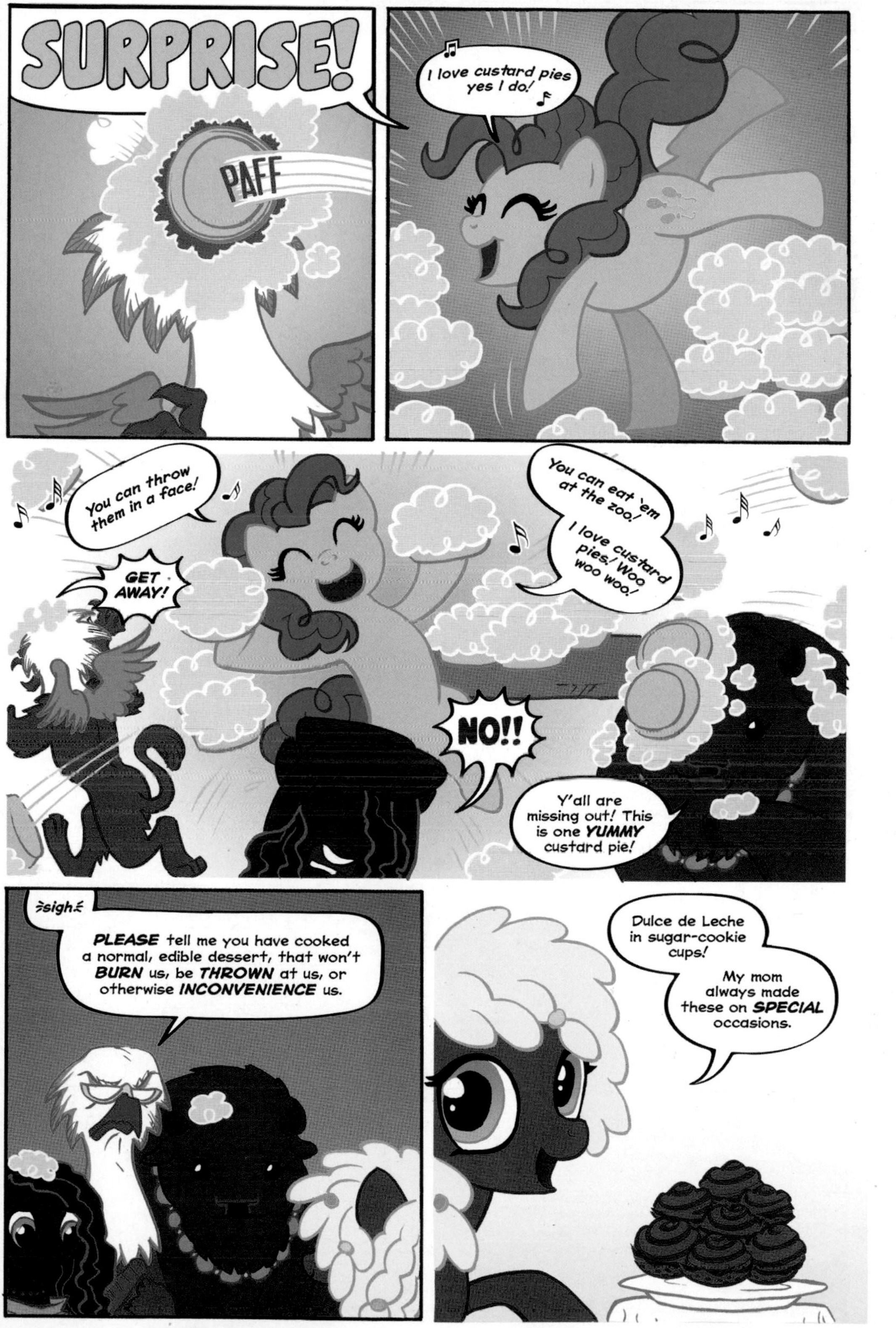

SURPRISE!
PAFF
I love custard pies yes I do!
You can throw them in a face!
GET AWAY!
You can eat 'em at the zoo!
I love custard pies! Woo woo woo!
NO!!
Y'all are missing out! This is one YUMMY custard pie!
sigh
PLEASE tell me you have cooked a normal, edible dessert, that won't BURN us, be THROWN at us, or otherwise INCONVENIENCE us.
Dulce de Leche in sugar-cookie cups!
My mom always made these on SPECIAL occasions.

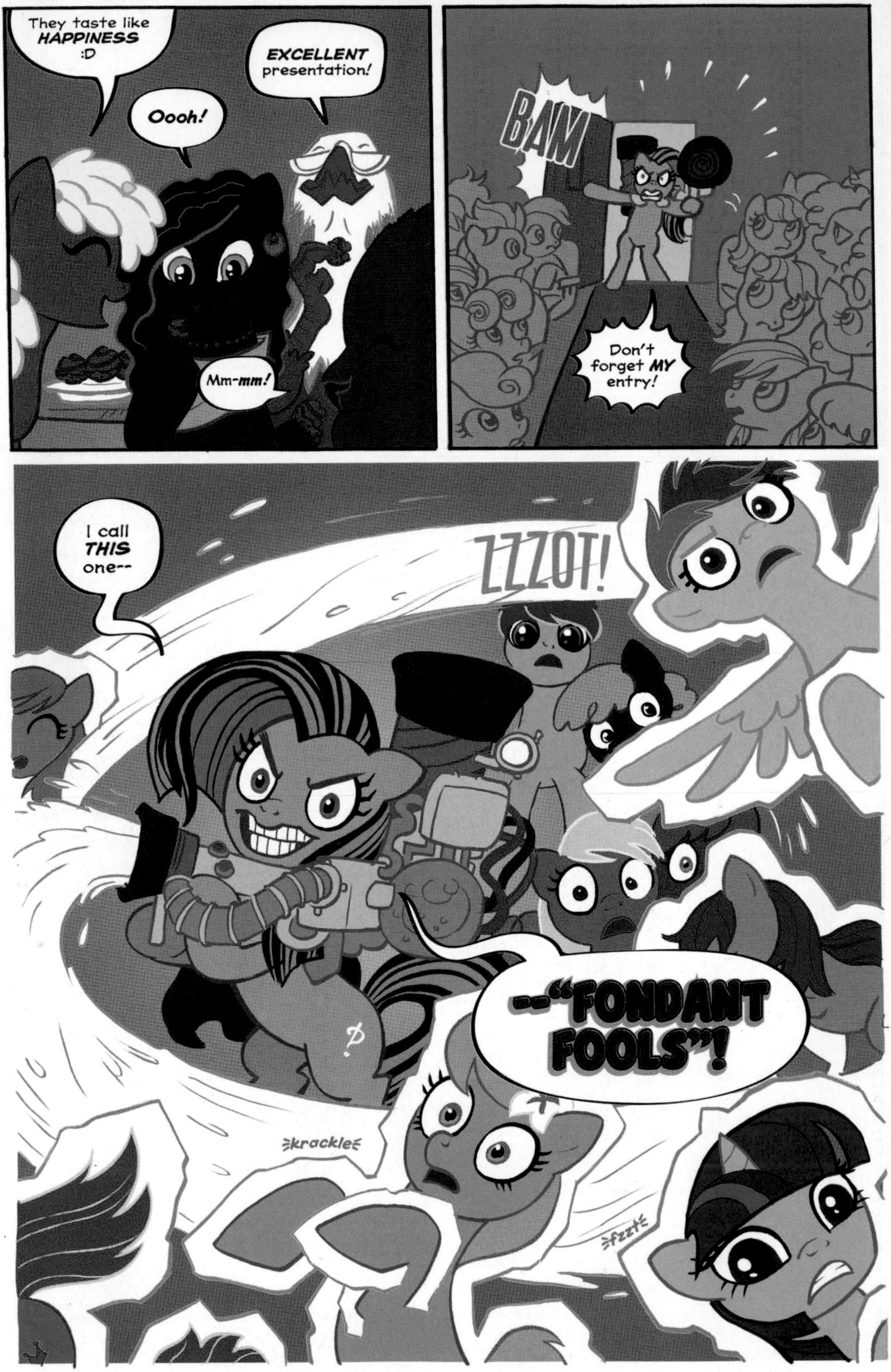
They taste like HAPPINESS :D
EXCELLENT presentation!
Oooh!
Mm-mm!
BAM
Don't forget MY entry!
I call THIS one--
ZZZOT!
--"FONDANT FOOLS"!
krackle
fzzt

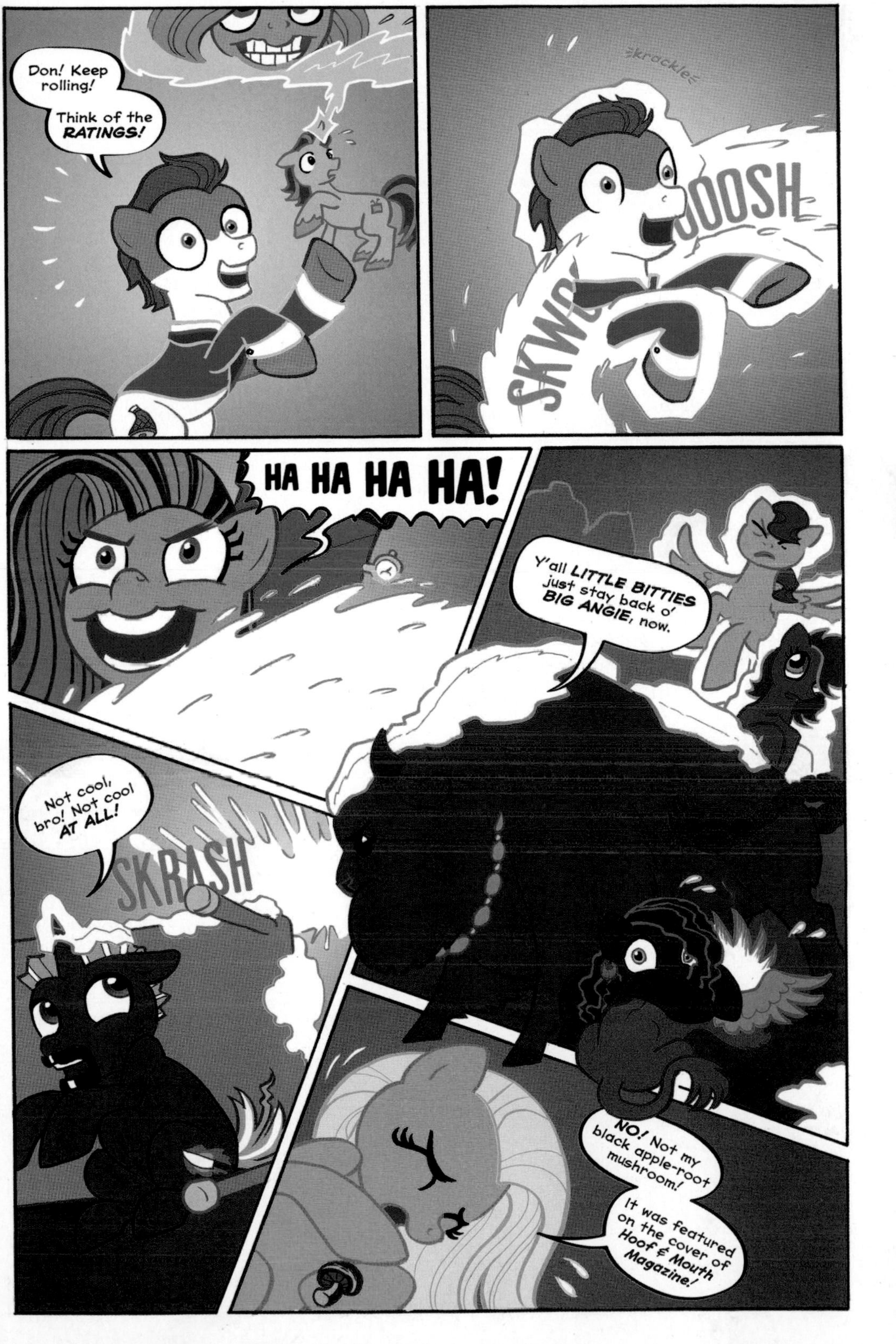
Don! Keep rolling!
Think of the RATINGS!
krackle
SKWEE
OOOSH
HA HA HA HA!
Y'all LITTLE BITTIES just stay back o' BIG ANGIE, now.
Not cool, bro! Not cool AT ALL!
SKRASH
NO! Not my black apple-root mushroom!
It was featured on the cover of Hoof & Mouth Magazine!

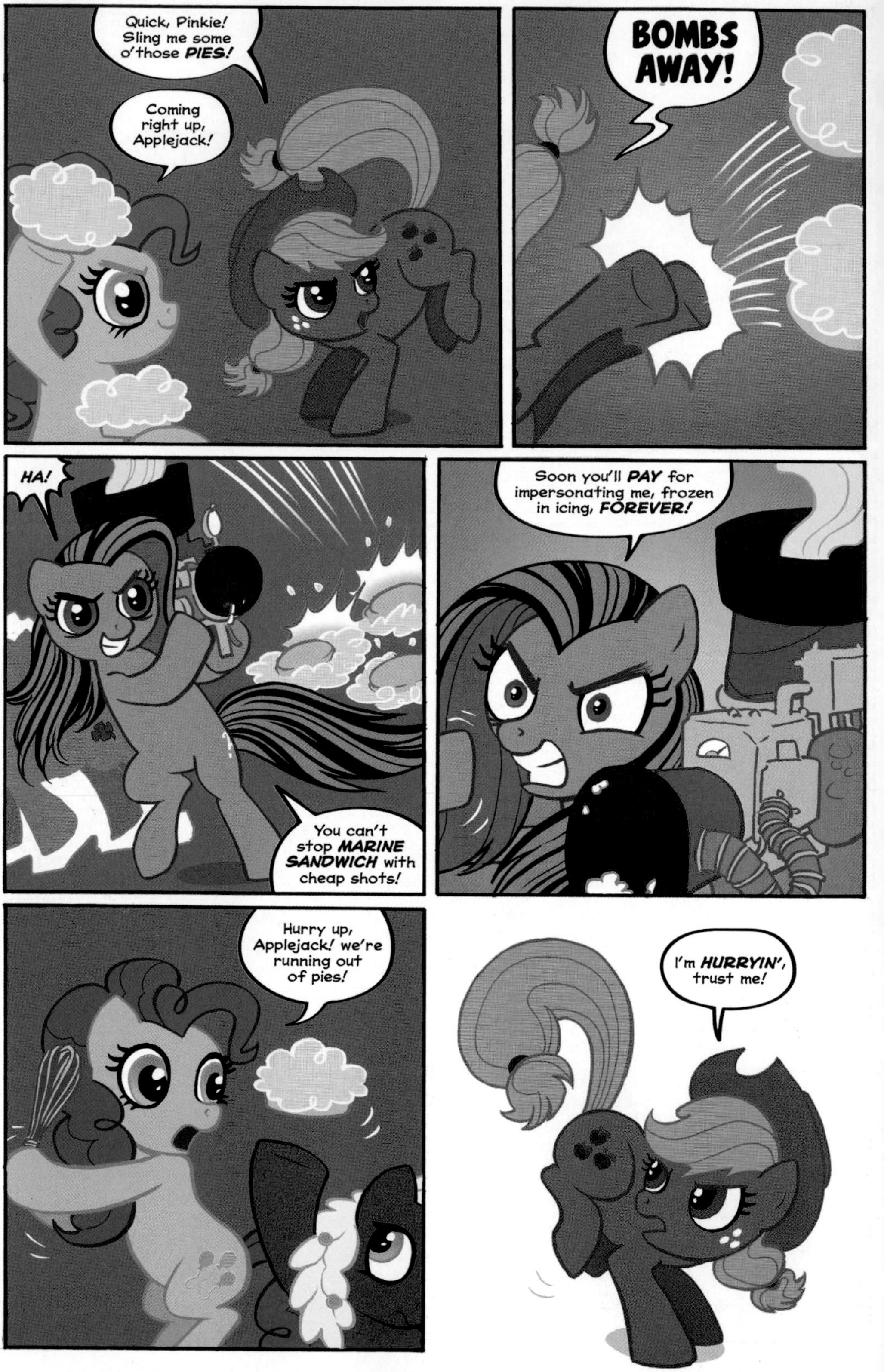

Quick, Pinkie! Sling me some o'those PIES!
Coming right up, Applejack!
BOMBS AWAY!
HA!
You can't stop MARINE SANDWICH with cheap shots!
Soon you'll PAY for impersonating me, frozen in icing, FOREVER!
Hurry up, Applejack! we're running out of pies!
I'm HURRYIN', trust me!

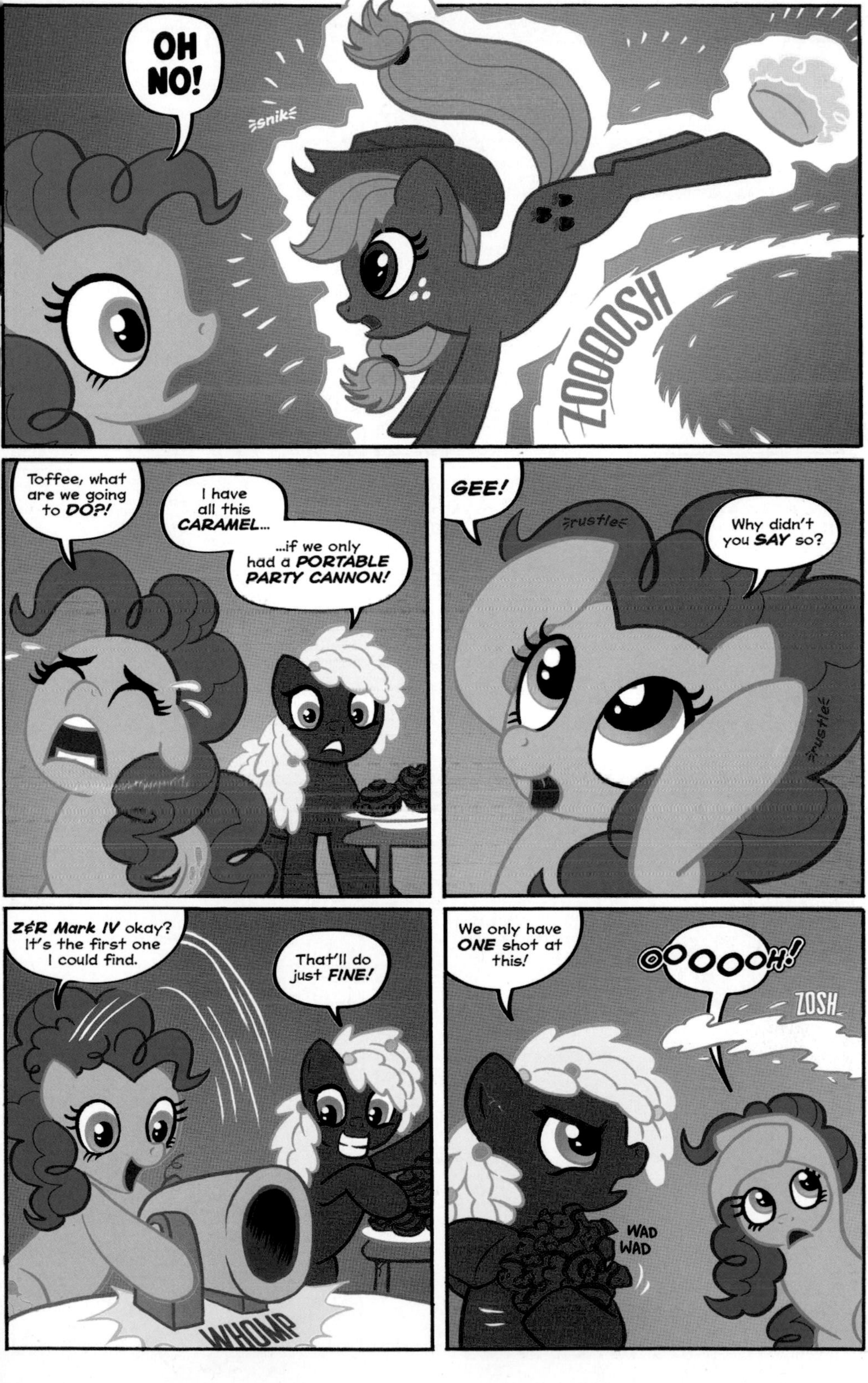
OH NO!
snik
ZOOOOOSH
Toffee, what are we going to DO?!
I have all this CARAMEL...
...if we only had a PORTABLE PARTY CANNON!
GEE!
rustle
Why didn't you SAY so?
rustle
Z&R Mark IV okay? It's the first one I could find.
That'll do just FINE!
WHOMP
We only have ONE shot at this!
OOOOOOH!
ZOSH
WAD WAD

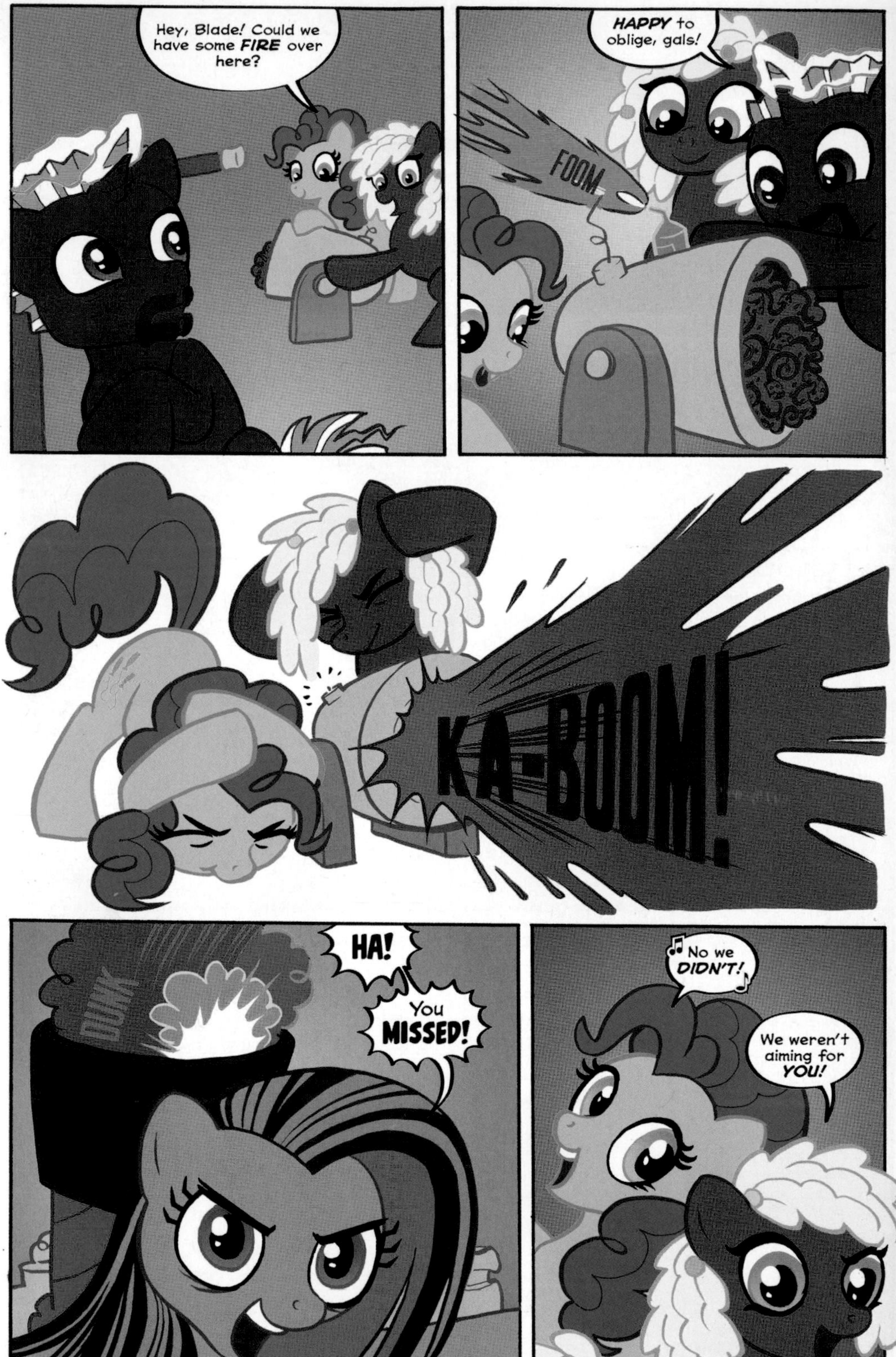

Hey, Blade! Could we have some FIRE over here?
HAPPY to oblige, gals!
FOOM
KA-BOOM!
DUNK
HA!
You MISSED!
No we DIDN'T!
We weren't aiming for YOU!

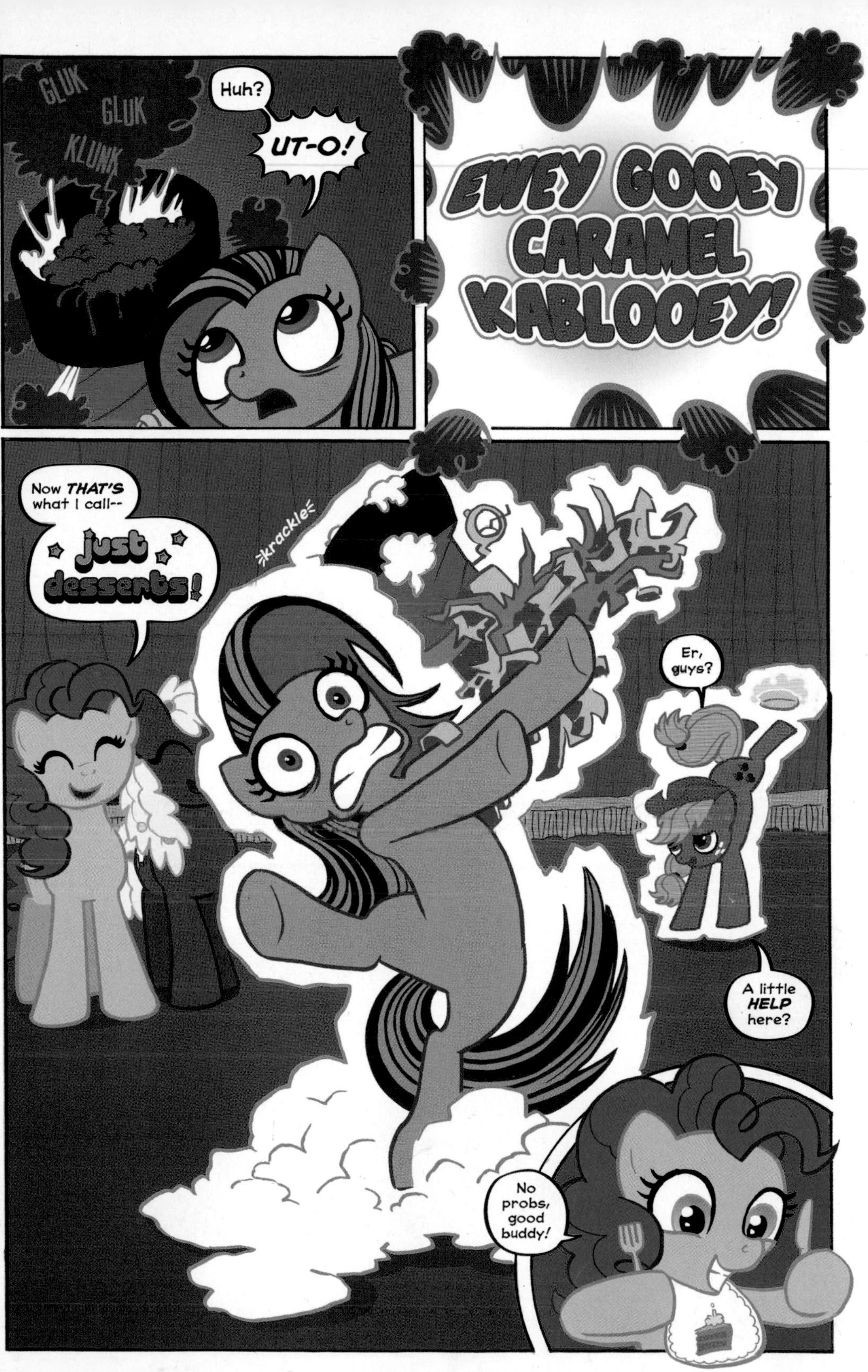
GLUK
GLUK
KLUNK
Huh?
UT-O!
EWEY GOOEY CARAMEL KABLOOEY!
Now THAT'S what I call--
just desserts!
krackle
Er, guys?
A little HELP here?
No probs, good buddy!

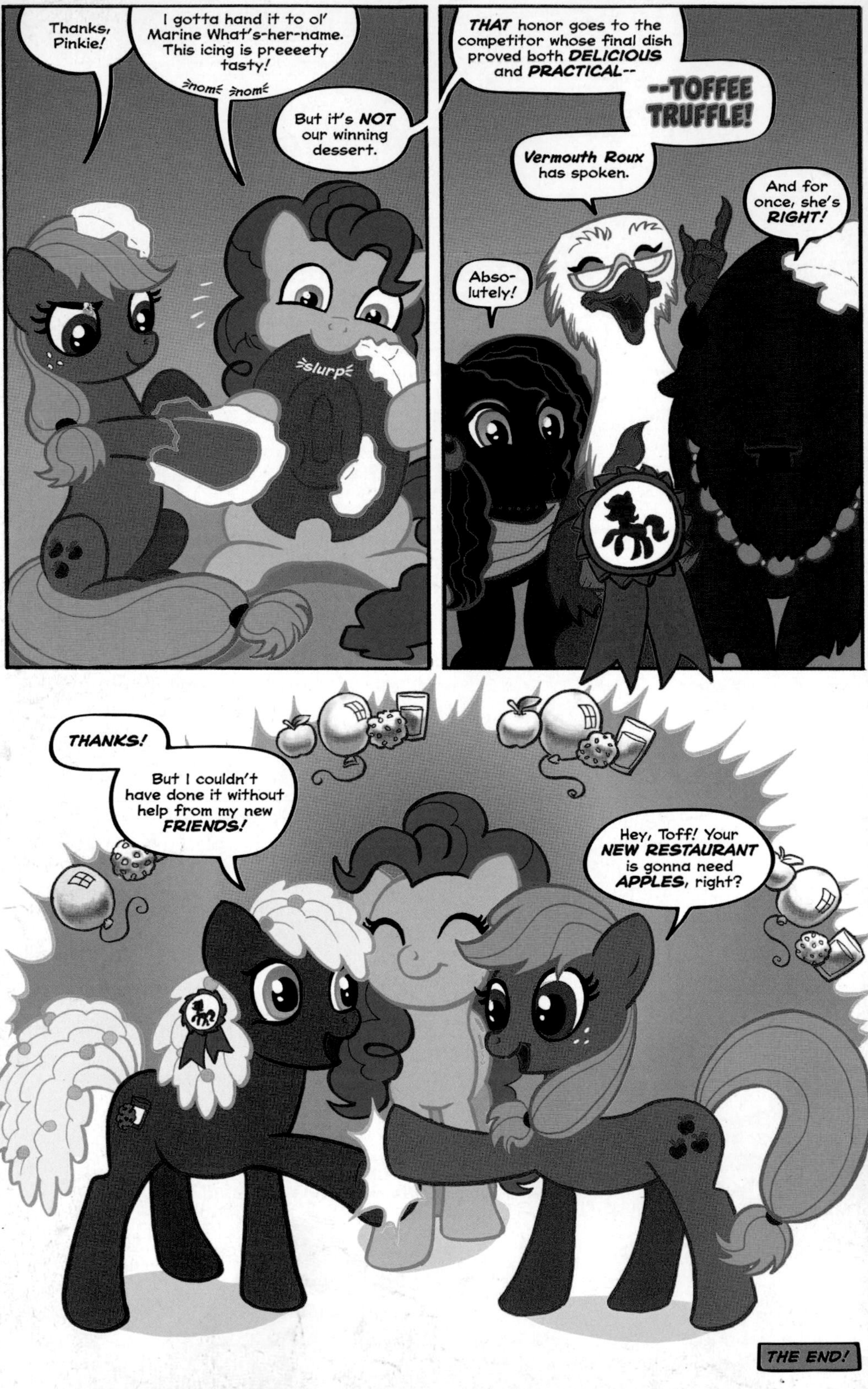
Thanks, Pinkie!
I gotta hand it to ol' Marine What's-her-name. This icing is preeeety tasty!
nom nom
slurp
But it's NOT our winning dessert.
THAT honor goes to the competitor whose final dish proved both DELICIOUS and PRACTICAL--
--TOFFEE TRUFFLE!
Vermouth Roux has spoken.
And for once, she's RIGHT!
Abso-lutely!
THANKS!
But I couldn't have done it without help from my new FRIENDS!
Hey, Toff! Your NEW RESTAURANT is gonna need APPLES, right?
THE END!

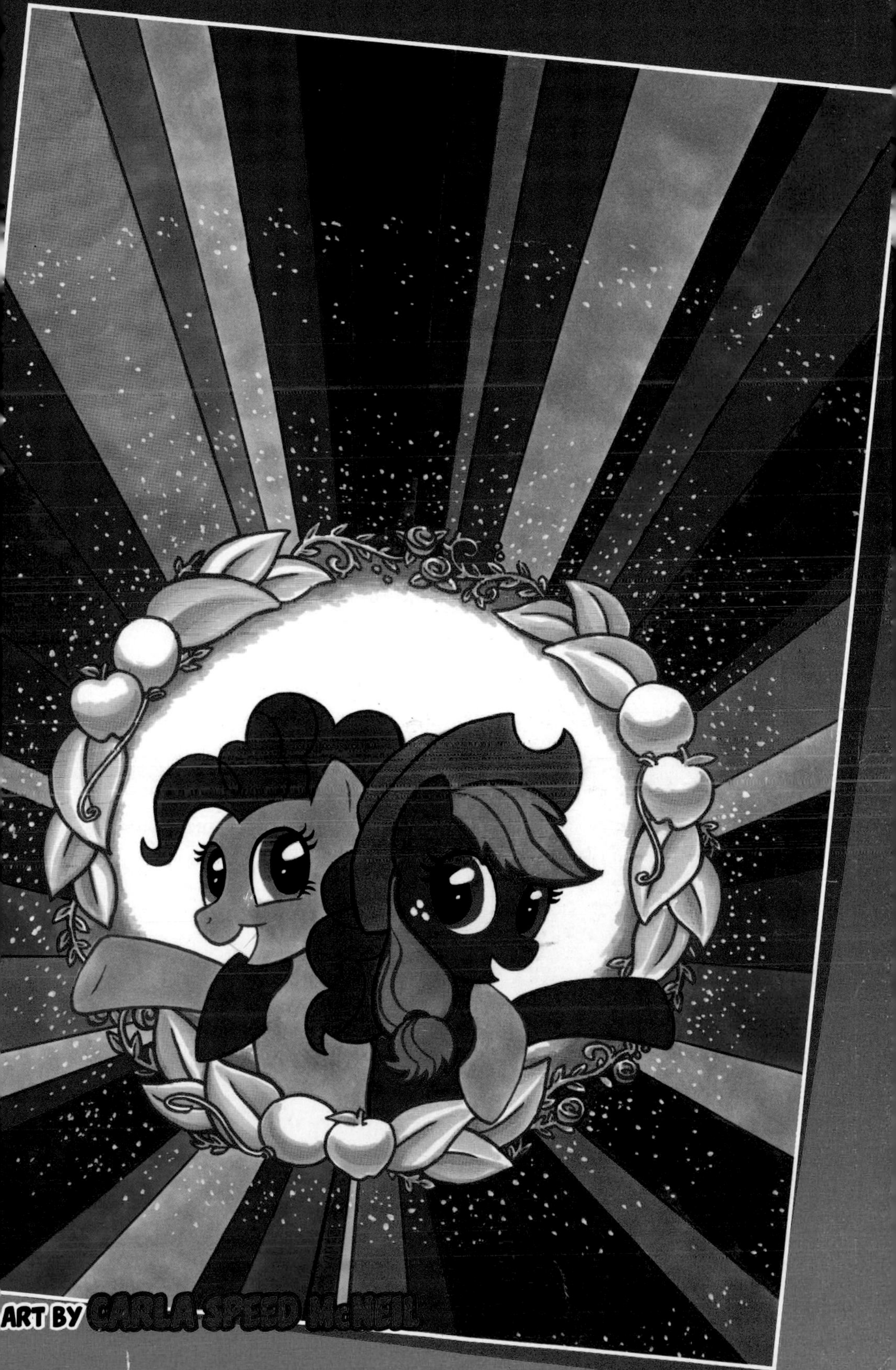

ART BY CARLA SPEED McNEIL

My Little Pony: Friendship Is Magic, Vol. 1
ISBN: 978-1-61377-605-6

My Little Pony: Pony Tales, Vol. 1
ISBN: 978-1-61377-740-4

My Little Pony: The Magic Begins
ISBN: 978-1-61377-754-1

These collections on sale now!

Licensed By:

IDW®   Hasbro

www.idwpublishing.com